The Hidde

MW00946920

Finale

B.M. Hardin

Copyright©2016

Savvily Published LLC

ISBN-13:
978-1537327044

ISBN-10:
1537327046

This book is a work of fiction. All persons, events, places and locales are a product of the others imagination. The story is fictitious and any thoughts of similarities are merely coincidental.

Dedication

This book is dedicated to all of my loyal and dedicated readers! Thank you all for your support and for following me on my writing journey. It is truly a blessing to have supporters like you in my corner. Thank you!

Acknowledgements

First and foremost, I want to thank my Heavenly Father for my talents and my gifts and each and every story that he has placed in me. It is an honor and a privilege to be living my dream and walking in my purpose and for that I am forever thankful.

Also to all of my family, friends, critiques, supporters, readers and everyone else, thank you for believing in me and allowing me to share my gifts with you.

Your support truly means the world to me!

B.M. Hardin

Author B.M. Hardin's contact info:

Facebook: http://www.facbook.com/authorbm

Twitter: @BMHardin1

Instagram: @bm_hardin

Email:bmhardinbooks@gmail.com

TEXT BMBOOKS to 22828 for Release updates!

THE HIDDEN WIFE 2

Prologue: Recap of Part ONE

My goodness, how many wives had he had?

"So, I was just what? Something to do?"

"No. You were an opportunity."

I felt myself getting angry but I knew that if I flipped out, he would probably shut down.

"An opportunity for what?"

"To do what we always do."

He said we. So, he and Brian must have had some type of plan from the very beginning.

"And what's that?"

"It doesn't matter. The problem is that I haven't done my part. I always do my part. And then I saw him, our son, my son, and I just wanted to be a part of his life. I wanted to be his dad. I wanted to be the dad that I never had."

"Wait, I thought your parents were married."

"My mother is doing life in prison and I never met my father. Those folks that you spoke to were friends. They owed me a few favors."

He just lied about everything!

So that's why none of his "family" made it to the wedding. He didn't have any.

"What are you saying Tobias?"

"I'm saying that I have to come up with a plan. We have to come up with a new plan."

"What do you mean we?"

"Like I said we."

"I have nothing to do with whatever you are talking about."

"Trust me. You have everything to do with it."

I started yelling at him and telling him that I hated that I ever met him and that he was the worst mistake of my life. I told him that he could take his plan and shove it up his skinny, black ass!

I didn't know what he was involved in and I didn't care what happened to him. I just wanted him out of my life. And I wanted him out now!

"Why can't you just go? Please just go."

"I'm not leaving behind my son. I just can't."

"He won't miss, who he doesn't know. If you leave now, he won't know you, and he will be just fine."

"I can't leave him. He's my second chance."

Huh?

"I had a son once."

"What?"

"I had a son."

"Had? I thought you said that you didn't have any kids Tobias."

"I don't. But I did."

I stared at him as he stared off into space.

"I took my eye off of him for a second. One little second. He was two years old and curious. I was the one that wanted the house by the lake. I was unloading the truck. I took my eye off of him. When I turned back around, he was gone. I checked the house, hoping that maybe he had gone inside but he wasn't there. My heart skipped a beat as I headed to the backyard. I saw his little hand come up out of the water as if he had been trying to swim. So I went running. I still remember how bad my eyes burned as I looked for him in the water. I found him, but I was too late. I tried to bring him back, but I was too late."

I fought back tears. I couldn't imagine. I had no idea. Why wouldn't he have told me something like that?

"Where was his mother?"

"She wasn't there. But she never fully forgave me for it. But I couldn't bring him back and I didn't want to replace him either. So, I refused to get any woman pregnant again. I always used protection, and then, I made the mistake with you. I was trying to fix it. I was hoping that you lost it, every single day. But you didn't. And now that he's coming, it just changes some things. Not all things, but some."

"Why are you telling me all of the Tobias? Why?"

He took a deep breath.

"Because if I don't figure out something…"

"What?"

"If I don't figure out a plan Tiffany…you're going to die."

What?

I looked at his face and he looked as though he was sure of it.

Die? How, why, was I going to die?

Just as I opened up my mouth, the lights flickered, and then they clicked off. The house was dark except the light from the moon shining in over the front door, making the room visible.

"Oh shit. She's here," Tobias said, as he walked closer to me.

"What? Who's here?" I asked as he grabbed my hand.

Out of nowhere, I heard what sounded like a chainsaw and then I watched it come through the front door, just above the door knob.

What in the hell?

"Who's here Tobias? Who's here?"

"My wife," he said, grabbing my hand and pulling me in the opposite direction.

What? What the hell did he mean *his wife*?

****

Chapter One

"What do you mean your wife?" I questioned Tobias, screaming over the sound of the chainsaw.

He didn't answer me. He just kept pulling me towards the back door. I tried to pull away from him, but he tightened his grip.

"What the hell is going on Tobias! And let go of me!" I pulled away from him again, but he got aggressive. The way that he pulled me towards him almost made me pee on myself.

"Tobias!"

"Shut up! I'm trying to get you out of here alive."

What the hell is that supposed to mean?

Unsure of what to think, I did as I was told. With me no longer resisting, Tobias finally managed to get me out of the back door. I could still hear the chainsaw as we stood on the side of the house. My heart was racing and I felt as though I was in one of those horror movies where all of the black people die first.

Finally, the chainsaw silenced, and Tobias waited for only a second before pulling me towards his car.

"Get in," he whispered as he hurried around to the other side. Once we were both inside of the car, without hesitating, he reversed it, knocked down the mailbox, and then sped down the street. I looked back towards the house but I didn't see anyone; accept for one of my neighbors' who must have gotten curious about all of the noise.

Tobias drove in silence. I could tell that he was nervous. He glanced at his phone. It was ringing over and over again. But he never answered it.

"Who is that? Who is that on the phone?"

Tobias didn't respond.

"Who was that at the house?"

Still, he ignored me.

"What the hell is going on Tobias? Who is that calling? Who was that at the house? Tell me! I swear if you don't start talking, right now, I'm going to jump out of this car, walk back home and ask whoever that was my damn self!"

We stopped at a red light and I opened the door.

"Shut the damn door Tiffany! Shut the door!"

He tried to reach over me but I shut the door, hard, just as the light turned green.

"Then tell me what's going on Tobias. What did you mean that *she* was, well, is your wife? I'm your wife."

"Not my real one."

What?

He pulled over on the side of the road and turned on his blinkers. Out of nowhere, I remembered that I had the gun in my purse. At this point, I didn't know what to think, but there was one thing that I could be sure of and that was that if he even thought about trying something crazy, I was going to blow his ass all the way to the land of *Oz*.

"I'm not your real what?"

"Wife. You're not my real wife."

"What? You're married to both of us? Is that what you're saying?" Impatiently, I waited for him to respond. I swallowed hard, as if I was trying to digest his comment. "What does that mean Tobias? Huh? I don't get what you're saying to me right now!"

"She's my *real* wife. The one that I'm married to under my real name. The only one that knows the real me. We've been married for years. Hell, almost twenty."

"Hold on, what the hell are you saying to me right now?"

"I'm saying that you are married to someone else's husband. I'm saying that the crazy lady back at your house, with the chainsaw, was, is, my wife, and she wasn't coming to talk."

My mouth was hanging wide open, but nothing came out of it. He has another wife? Wait, he's saying that he's still married to someone else, while he's married to me? That can't possibly be what he's saying to me! I was confused and he had a hell of a lot of explaining to do!

"Damn it!" Tobias shook his head.

"So, I mean what the hell was this? What, everything was just some big, twisted lie? You lied to me and had a wife the whole time? That's what you're saying right?"

"Look. We don't have time to talk about that right now, Strawberry. I messed up. And if I can't figure out something, she's going to do something crazy."

"To who?"

"To you. She wouldn't hurt me. But she could care less about you."

"What is that supposed to mean? I didn't do anything, to anybody! What the hell do I have to do with all of this?"

"Everything."

"Like what? You lied to me, just like I'm sure that you've been lying to her."

"I've never lied to her," he said honestly.

Huh? Now I was even more confused!

"So you haven't been lying to her and creeping around with me?"

"No."

"If you've been married to her the whole time Tobias, where in the hell has she been?"

"Around. She has always been around."

"And she knows that you are "married" to me too? If I can even call it that."

"Yes. Of course she does. She's the one that found you. She's the one that told me that you were the right one."

"The right one? For what?"

Tobias looked at me.

"For what damn it!"

"The right opportunity. The lonely ones are easier."

I analyzed his words. I thought about his recent actions and the papers that he'd tricked me into signing. I knew exactly what this was all about.

"So, wait a minute. You married me for my money, didn't you?"

"Isn't that obvious by now? It damn sure wasn't for love. At least not at first. But as of now, I can't honestly say that I don't feel something for you. Hell, after I play the part for a while, naturally, I start to feel something for the women involved. But it never amounts to what I feel for her. That is, until, you started carrying my child. It just changed everything. It changed my thoughts. My feelings. It changed my plans."

I felt like I was going to be sick. I rolled down the window and touched my stomach. I could feel Tobias looking at me; watching me in concern. He damn sure didn't need to be worried about me. He was the one in danger and he didn't even know it.

Tobias started driving so that I could get a good breeze. I wanted to cry but I couldn't. Or maybe it was that I wouldn't. But I still wanted more. He still owed me more.

"Start talking. I want to know everything. I want you to break this down for me. Explain this bull crap to me Tobias," I said in between breaths.

"What else is there to explain Tiffany?"

"Everything! I want to know everything. If you ever want to see your son, I suggest you start talking. Hell, you seem to care about him so damn much, I'll go right back to that abortion clinic and finish what I should've done the first time. Even if I am over the weeks, I'm sure that's nothing that dollar signs can't fix. So, if you want this baby, you better tell me everything. And it better be the truth too!"

I didn't look at him, but I knew that he knew that I meant business. But I was lying. I wouldn't dare get rid of my baby now, but he didn't know that.

"Everybody wants the truth, but can they handle it? My mama went to prison when I was thirteen. After that, I moved around a lot. Whoever would take me in, that's where I went. Whoever would be fine with getting the checks and food stamps that came along with keeping me for a while, and then I'll be out of a place to stay again. So, after a while, I started making my own way. I started getting into trouble. I picked up some bad habits. I tried to do what I could to get money. To make sure that I at least ate every day. Stealing, gambling, you name it, I did it. Eventually, it caught up with me."

His tone in his voice was different. It wasn't so educated or intelligent, yet it felt authentic. Natural. As if he'd said to hell with pretending.

"*She* was a runaway. She left home when she was fifteen because her Daddy couldn't keep his hands to himself. Her trifling-ass mama never even came to look for her. Never even reported her missing. We checked into it years later. The streets taught her how to survive. She was tough. Rough around the edges, when I met her. But I liked it. It was just something about her. She saved my life. I'd turned into a little errand boy. But stealing from people was always something I was good at, so I started cutting corners, keeping a little extra. That shit caught up to me. I was getting my ass beat in the alley by Big Mike one day. She was working under the table for this Mexican Restaurant. They paid her with food and a few bucks to take out trash and wash dishes. She saw what was going on and tried to stop him. He pushed her down and then she came back with a brick. She hit him in the back of the head, twice, until he fell down. Big Mike was dead."

I didn't know what to say.

"She'd saved my life. Then I turned around and saved hers. She started to panic, but I told her to go back to work, and I got rid of the brick. I found out later that she had come back and poured some kind of chemical on his bloody fists to get rid of any traces of my DNA; before anyone found him. Then and there, I knew that we could have this Bonnie and Clyde type of thing. She was a little older than I was, but I had never had anybody to care about what happened to me. She did. And everything went from there. I've done some foul shit in my day. I ain't proud of most of it. And I should be in somebody's prison right about now. But she rolled with me through it all. I don't ever have to worry about her telling a soul. My secrets are safe with her. And hers are safe with me. I love her. Always have. My queen. Her king," he glanced at me as though he thought that maybe that was a bit much to say. It seemed as though he actually loved her the way that he pretended to love me.

"We did whatever we had to do to survive. We found what jobs we could for a while. We moved over and over again. We went wherever my beat up Chevy would take us. Looking for more. Looking for better. I didn't have anybody and neither did she. Once we had each other to lean on, we tried to do things the right way. We did. But money was always tight. And then..."

Tobias breathed heavily.

"We met this couple; husband and wife. They were filthy rich too. He was some kind of celebrity plastic surgeon and she was from England and from a family full of money. One day, the husband spotted her coming out of a store. He wanted her. And the wife wanted to see if the "big dick black guy" stories were true. So they made us an offer. At first, I went off. Turned the parking lot out. Tried to give that rich white man the *business.* But she calmed me down and got me to see the bigger picture. Money. We needed money."

I almost laughed, but not because I found something funny. I felt like that was the only thing that I could do to keep me from blacking out and going in my purse. My finger on that trigger would feel pretty damn good right about now!

"They offered us $2500 just to have sex with them. One night."

"Swingers?"

"I guess that's what they were. We didn't bother to ask. At first we thought that they were kidding, but quickly they proved to us that they weren't. He wrote the check and put it in my hand. All we had to do was do the deed and then we could cash it. I wanted to skip out on the deal and run to the bank, but I was sure that by the time we got there, they would have canceled it. We needed that money. If I'm not mistaken, we had about $85 to our names and had been sharing food for over a week to try to make the money stretch. Neither of us could remember the last time that we'd gone to sleep on a full stomach. The check was right there in my hand. The money was just a stroke, pump, orgasm away. So, together, we did what we had to do. We made the swap."

I shook my head.

"Rich folks always have the darkest secrets or some crazy ass fantasies, don't they? We swapped, but the wife had an agenda of her own. She asked if we could make a little arrangement. She wanted to keep getting the dick behind her husband's back. And she was willing to keep paying for it too. As I said, I've never lied to my wife. I told her what was up and she told me to do it. She said that it was just sex, it didn't mean anything. She even made a joke saying that I was looking for work…and I'd just found a job. Selling dick. Ain't that some shit?"

I didn't even answer his question. Obviously his wife was missing a few marbles. And hell, maybe he was too.

"I knew then that she was willing to do anything to survive. Anything to get us to where we wanted to be. So, Nevi, the married English woman, and I fooled around for a while. She liked the thrill of sneaking around. I liked cashing those checks. But after so long, she wanted something else. She wanted me."

Tobias entered the highway, and I wondered where in the hell he was taking me.

"She fell in love with me; or maybe it was with the ding-a-ling; either way, she wanted me all to herself. She left her husband and asked me to leave my wife. She told me that I would never have to worry about money or work again. All I had to do was be with her. But I couldn't. I actually loved my wife. I couldn't leave her. I've never been able to. Never really had a reason to," Tobias admitted.

His wife, the real one, was a damn fool! Even more of a fool than I was! No husband of mine, knowingly, is selling or slanging dick, to any other woman, but me.

His phone vibrated, but he continued to talk.

"She'd saved my life. In more ways than one. After I met her, it was like I had someone to care about other than myself. And her loyalty made me love her even more. If we had to sleep in the car, she made the best of it. If we were hungry, she didn't mind going to steal us a pack of meat. And she never left. Through the hard times, she stayed. As pretty as she is, there were plenty of men who wanted her. But she wanted me. So, with the proposition from Nevi on the table, instead of telling me to drop her, my wife helped me realize that Nevi was an opportunity. A way out. Nevi wanted me. But what about what I wanted? What about what we needed? We needed money. Nevi had the money. Nevi wanted me. So, why not let her have me...too?"

Tobias waited to see if I had any questions or comments but I remained silent. Finally, he started talking again.

"Brian."

Brian? So they did know each other before all of this? I couldn't wait to hear what he was about to say next.

"I've known Brian just as long as I've known myself. To keep it real with you, our mothers went to prison, together, for the same crime. They killed his step-father."

Wait…what?

"Brian's mother isn't in prison."

"Yes she is. The woman that finished raising him is his aunt. He just calls her Mama."

What! I was pretty sure that my sister didn't know that! Thinking of her, immediately I wished that I would have stayed at the hospital.

"Her husband used to beat her. She never reported it. She never told anyone but my mama. Everyone knows that you need something on record, especially if you're about to try to get away with a murder. But nevertheless, he jumped on her one night and they killed him. They thought that they would get away with it, but they didn't. Being that they had talked about it, it seemed premeditated. They didn't even give them self-defense. Both of them got thirty years in prison. I was thirteen when I watched them take my mama away and I ain't seen her since. Not once."

I remembered him saying that his friends were acting like his mother and sister and that he was lying about having family that was coming to our wedding. Everything that he'd ever told me was a lie. It was all lies.

"Brian and I lost touch, naturally. I'd moved thousands of miles away from where I'd grown up. But I knew where to find him. And I did. I remembered that he could do anything, everything, with a computer. He was damn near a genius. His IQ was so damn high, that the teachers used to second guess themselves and ask him questions."

There's the connection. Brian knew everything the whole time.

"My wife had this idea. She said that sex was okay, but all women want love. What if I could give Nevi love? At least make her think that's what it was. What if I could give her marriage? I would have access to everything. All of her money would be at my disposal. I could get as much as I could out of her and be set for life if I played my cards right. What if I could be two husbands at once? Temporarily two different men? Just for a while. Just long enough to get what we needed out of Nevi."

"So you scam women into marrying you. Get rich off of them, and then spend their money on and with another woman?"

"Precisely. Hell, everybody uses somebody. It may be in a different way. It may be for different reasons or for different things. But everyone gets used and everyone uses someone else."

He may be on to something there.

"My first fake name came from some show I'd watched on TV. I told Nevi that she'd been calling me a nickname the whole time. Gave her a name and that's where Brian came into the mix. After tracking him down, I asked him if he could do it; make me someone else, and he laughed in my face. Of course he could. He made me a new identity. He gave me a social security number, birth certificate, new parents, and all kinds of credentials. He even knew how to do some weird thing with my finger prints. Whoever I am at the time, my fingerprints, match; at least electronically. I got arrested on purpose, once, just to see. It was like I was a totally different man. His services don't come cheap though. If you must know, that's where the $50,000 that I took out of the bank went. And I'm one of his least expensive clients. He does things like this for people more than you know. Big people. That whole little, "he got a new job" gathering, was bullshit. Brian is a smart, dangerously smart man. But that's none of my business."

I didn't want to believe him. But I did. I knew that everything that Tobias was saying was true.

"It was only supposed to be a one-time thing; marry Nevi and take her money. Then go on with my life and wife. But one turned into two and then you. You are *fake-wife* number 3."

I breathed deeply, slowly. I was so overwhelmed. I felt like I was having one of my terrible nightmares, but I knew that I wasn't. I was wide awake and this mess was my life. This man that was talking was my fake husband and had really been out to take from me and use me. I felt like needles were stuck in my throat. I felt like…nothing.

I guess Karma had finally found me and she wasn't taking it easy on me either. And the sad part was that I had a feeling that she wasn't through with me yet. She was just getting started.

"Everything worked just like we planned. I changed my identity and after a few months, I talked Nevi into marrying me. She'd had me sign a prenuptial agreement, so I knew that I had to get as much money as I could from her while we were married. And I did. I would remind her of what she told me and she would give me money, time and time again. She actually had an account that I had access to. She would ask questions here and there but I would say that

I was investing or that I was working on something, but I was taking the money and giving it to my real wife for her to stash it away. After a long while, and once Nevi started to complain, I knew it was time for me to get out of it. It was time for me to go. I was just going to disappear. Hell she was married to a man that didn't exist anyway. But I'll be damned if she didn't make her move first. She'd divorced me so fast that even I didn't see it coming. I woke up one morning and she had the papers lying on the pillow beside me. She told me to sign them and have my shit out of her house before she got back from England. But it was all good. I had what I wanted and we had what we needed. For the hell of it I signed the papers. The "divorce" was quiet, fast and with it all over, I went back to my wife. And life was good for a long while. For years we were okay. But one day we woke up and realized, that the money was almost gone. We'd spent big in the beginning. Trips. Gambling. Shopping. But we cracked down fast and pinched off of it as long as we could. And then one day, she suggested that we do it again. Hell, we'd gotten away with it the first time. She even offered to marry some old rich geezer that was near death, take all his money and then come back to me. But I didn't want another man touching her. By then I was older, and nobody was going to screw my wife but me."

Well, what kind of crap is that? If that isn't a double standard, then I don't know what is!

"So it was on me. Find some lonely, rich, desperate woman, and show her the best few months of her life, get her to trust me. Marry her. After that, the rest would be a breeze. All I needed was access to her money. So, we did it again. We found me another fake *wife*. She wasn't as rich as the first one, but she had a good bit of money and she was all alone. But with that wife, things went all wrong."

Tobias finally answered the phone and said these words: "Stop. Yes. No. Okay."

I wasn't sure what was said on the other end of the phone but those were his only responses.

"What went wrong?"

"That wife ended up dead."

My heart skipped a beat.

"Who killed her?"

"She did," he said, nodding his head towards his phone.

Fear took over my body and I shifted in my seat as Tobias sped down the highway.

"Why?" He looked at me. "Why did she kill her?"

"Because she loved me; by "she" I'm referring to, Amber, fake-wife #2. No matter what I did to her, she wouldn't leave me. She had plenty of money but she was a little more attentive. I couldn't just take and take without her noticing. During the dating stage, I'd tried to test the limits and she let it be known that she was watching. So, I had to go another route. I got her to sign a paper, just like I did to you. If she wanted a divorce, she had to buy me out. Being hands on with the wedding plans, made it easy to get the signatures I needed."

Same mess he'd tried to pull on me! But he wasn't getting a dime of my money!

"How hard can it be to force a woman to a divorce? I gave her a month or two after the wedding of marital bliss and then I started to act out. But she didn't want to leave me. She didn't want to divorce me. She loved me so much and she tried to make our marriage work no matter what crazy foolishness I pulled on her. I even brought another woman into our home, in our bed, but that wasn't enough. She just suggested counseling. To be honest, after a while, I started to feel like shit for what I was doing to her. She was just too kind and too damn forgiving. And that was the problem. My real wife stepped in and tried to help speed up the process. She played on her phone. She did other little things to try to make Amber throw in the towel, but the poor woman just wouldn't let me go. So, she killed her."

These people are freaking crazy! I wondered if that was the case with me. That must have been why all of the crazy, random things had been happening. To force me into a divorce. To try to make me divorce Tobias so that he could try to take my money.

"I told her that I was going to handle it. I was just going to walk away and leave that poor woman alone, without taking her for all her money. Damn, I still have a heart. I felt bad. I tried to find another solution. I thought, maybe I would gamble a few thousands, get lucky, hit big, and we would never have to go through all of this again. So, I took a gambling trip. I told Amber that we had to talk when I got home but when I came back, Amber, was dead. My impatient ass *wife* had set the house on fire while she was asleep inside."

It amazed me that he would even put somebody in this situation, knowing what his real wife, as he called her, was capable of. It just showed how selfish he was.

"Aw hell, put your seat belt on."

Tobias was looking through the rearview mirror, and I turned around. There it was. The white Mercedes. The car was speeding in our direction and I looked at Tobias in a panic.

"The car isn't slowing down!"

"Of course not," he said, stretched his arm out in front of my stomach as the car rammed into us from behind.

"What the hell!"

Tobias seemed to be somewhat grinning, as he switched lanes. The car got behind us.

"Is that her? Is that your wife?"

"Yep."

She rammed her car into the back of Tobias's car again. I closed my eyes and shielded my belly.

"Hold on," Tobias said as he took an Exit in just the nick of time. The Mercedes hadn't been able to stop in time to make the Exit so it kept going."

"What was that! What the hell was that?"

"Her. I told you. She has a temper."

Tobias headed down the road and entered another highway.

"She's just pissed off. Don't worry about her."

"Don't worry about her? Really? Don't worry about her?"

"I can handle her."

"Apparently you can't! She killed one of your little pretend-wives already! I'm sure that she won't mind killing another!"

"You're different. I'll make sure that she doesn't hurt you. You're carrying my child. I'll die trying to protect him."

I didn't know what to say, so for the rest of the ride, I didn't say anything. I didn't even ask him where we were going. I found out once we pulled up at a hotel.

"I want you to stay here. Just for tonight. I promise you, you're going to be fine. I just need to talk to her."

I just looked at him. I didn't say a word. I guess I was trying to figure out if all of this was really happening or not. Tobias got out of the car and disappeared for a few minutes. Finally, he came back out and reached me a hotel key.

"Just for tonight. You can go back home tomorrow."

Like hell I can! I didn't know where I was going but there was no way in hell that I was going home!

"Which wife was the old lady talking about? At the restaurant that day? Your real wife? And what's her name Tobias?"

"No. Not my real wife. We are never, ever, seen together when I'm "on the job". The old lady was talking about another woman that I was going to make my fake-wife, before you, but we discovered that she wasn't as wealthy as we'd thought. So I left her two weeks before the wedding. Then we found you."

I noticed that he'd avoided telling me his wife's name.

"My real wife and I never cross paths, publicly, until the job is over. No one ever sees us together, or even speaking for that matter. But she's always, somewhere, watching."

"Is she your maid Isabelle?"

"There was never a maid Strawberry. And that wasn't my house. I was renting. And yes, that was her that night by the pool. As I said, she's always, somewhere. Watching."

Unbelievable!

"But why Tobias? You have your own money. I saw it. You had enough to invest. Why bother me? You have your own money."

"The money you saw was the last of the life insurance policy that I'd collected from Amber's death. That's the last of it. What, it might've carried us for another year or two. Depending on what state we ended up in. We just needed a little more. As a crutch. You were going to be the last one. I swear. Not only because it was getting old, but being around you made me different. You were different from the first two. You made me want to be more. I mean, I had to play the part. I had to look like I had something else to offer you other than my dick. I had to look and talk like money. Look and talk like you. The others had money, but it was inherited money. You were the V.I.P of a company. So, I had to step to you correct. Their wealth was given to them so in my opinion, they were weak. You'd earned yours. And anyone who meets you will know it. But I got you. I got you to fall for me. But I messed up. You weren't supposed to get pregnant."

I touched my stomach.

"I tried to make you have a miscarriage. I tried to stress you out, but the baby held on. She knew that a baby made things complicated; and she also knew that it was going to give me a soft spot for you that I didn't need to have. She was right. I don't want anything to happen to my son. The situation, is what it is, but that's still my son. My seed. My flesh and blood. She can't understand it. But she doesn't have to. It's my child."

The baby started to move as he tried to touch my stomach but I moved away.

"We used to pregnancy to trick you into marrying me so quickly, but we didn't expect it to be so hard for you to either lose it or to force you to want to get rid of it. And by the time that you wanted to have the abortion, I'd had a change of heart. And that really pissed her off. And so now, she wants you and the baby dead. At least the baby. She doesn't give a damn about what we initially planned. All she cares about is making sure that you don't have that baby. But there has to be a way. I can't let anything happen to my son."

Damn! What about me?

"When I saw him, moving around in there, I wanted to know him. I wanted to see his face and touch his fingers and toes. She's always wanted to have another child. But never. After all of these years, never has she been able to get pregnant again. I thought it was me. But clearly, it's not. What if this is my last chance at fatherhood?"

"Another child?"

"Yes. It was our son that drowned in the lake. The son I told you about. She never forgave me for his death. The news of your pregnancy damn near killed her. Hell, the iron that she threw at my head damn near killed me. She will never accept him. So you see my dilemma."

Tobias looked at his phone and then turned it to face me. It was a text message from a number that he didn't have saved in his phone. I tried to lock it into my memory, but the text message caused me to forget every single digit.

"I'm going to kill your little bitch and that baby! You can run, but you can't hide her forever!"

What in the hell was I going to do?

****

Chapter TWO

"Did she wake up yet?"

"No." My little sister April said.

"I'm not feeling too well. I can't come today. Maybe tomorrow."

"You okay?"

"I'm fine. Just please keep me posted."

She hung up without asking anything else or trying to find out more information like a normal person. I swear she's just so weird. I sat the phone on the dresser and I looked at myself in the hotel mirror.

Tobias convinced me to stay at the hotel for the night. I'd heard him and her go at it terribly on the phone before he left and it seemed as though Tobias was either scared of her; or worried that he wouldn't be able to control her. Either way, I needed to be as far away from their mess as possible. I'd spent all night crying and feeling sorry for myself. I felt like a fool. I mean, I had to be the second biggest dummy, because the first spot belonged to Tobias's real wife, in the world. I'm just saying.

But all of the red flags were there, prior to marrying him. Maybe not about this issue in particularly, but I'd known deep down that something was off. Something wasn't right. And now, everything was so clear. I should have listened to my gut. I shouldn't have listened to my sister. I should have listened to my heart.

I just couldn't believe that this was happening to me. I mean, sure, I'd come to accept the fact that Tobias was full of you know what, but never would I have imagined something like this. Never would I have imagined that he had been married to some woman, for years and that they were apart of some kind of scam or whatever they wanted to call it. Marrying wealthy women for their money. Using them, hurting them, hell even killing them. But they had the wrong one this time. They were about to find out that in actuality, they chose the wrong wife. I wasn't just going to roll over and let them kill me.

Oh no. I was working on a plan of my own.

I grabbed my purse and pulled out the gun. I started to think of different scenarios that might work. Different scenarios where I could "accidentally" or defensively, shoot Tobias and get away with it.

I've done worse. I've sent an innocent man to prison for falsely accusing him of rape, so my lying skills were on point. And my shooting skills were too.

Maybe I could provoke Tobias to attack me and then shoot him and say that it was self-defense. I needed a witness. Or some kind of incident on record to back me first. Yeah. That was the first step. All I had to do was put something on record.

But what about his "hidden" wife?

She was already out to get me and surely if I killed Tobias, I would have to kill her too. But okay. I was cool with that. Hell, she was going to get me if I didn't get her first anyway. With a thousand thoughts and scenarios floating around in my head, I screamed out in frustration.

Ugh! I just wanted my lonely, miserable, life back. That's it. I just wanted my life back. Being alone wasn't all that bad, especially compared to all of this. I might would've had more luck with that ugly blind date that my sister tried to set me up with. Ugly people usually make the best mates anyway. Hell, most of the time don't nobody want their ugly ass but you.

I placed the gun down and called Tobias but he didn't answer. I wasn't even sure why I'd called him in the first place. He couldn't be trusted. I couldn't even be sure if he was telling the truth about everything that he'd said. He'd been lying to me for this long. Why stop now? But if nothing else, he seemed to really care about the safety of the baby, so for now, that was the only thing that I had working in my favor.

I called my ex-husband Ray, but he didn't answer either. I sent him a 9-1-1 text message, and waited for his response. After a few minutes, and with neither of them getting back to me, feeling like a sitting duck, against Tobias wishes, I grabbed my purse and headed out of the hotel.

Hell, I was probably safer if he didn't know where I was anyway.

~***~

Tobias Speaks...

"Sit down!"

She ignored me. I stared at her. I stood up and walked over to her. I didn't have to put on some gentleman, proper act with her. She knew me. And she knew that I meant business.

"Didn't I tell you to shut up and sit down? Ain't that what I said? I told you I got this. I don't need your damn help! You're ruining everything! I got it! And you cut her damn door with a chainsaw, really? Dramatic as hell, don't you think?"

"Oh well! You should've answered your phone! I was going to cut that baby out of that bitch stomach myself!" she screamed in my face.

She hated the baby. There's no way she was ever going to accept him. I already knew this. But something was going to have to give.

"I got this okay?"

"No you don't! You don't "got it". She's still pregnant, with your baby! That baby has you confused! You're not sticking to the plan. We should've been gone by now. Just like we'd planned. So, you don't got it. But I do. I'm gonna' fix it, since you can't!"

"No, you're not going to do a damn thing but stay away from her and let me do what I do. Your problem is the baby. I get that but damn it! You know what, he's coming whether you like it or not! So get the fuck over it already! And you're not going to do anything to him, or…"

"Or what, huh? You're going to leave me?"

"I ain't say that."

"Or what then? Don't threaten me!"

"I'm not threatening you. I just want you to let me handle it. That's all. Hell, I told her enough to make her not want anything to do with me. Maybe she will give me the baby. Everything will be fine."

She looked at me.

"Do I look stupid to you? She's not going to give us her baby, dummy! I swear, I put this on my life, I won't stand by you if you don't do something. We've done it all, together, we've been through hell and back. But I'm not watching another woman have your child. I just can't do it."

"Look. Just hear me out. So what if she has the baby huh? You have my heart. You know that. Things are jacked up. This wasn't a part of the plan. But that's okay. Ain't nobody gotta' die; especially not my child. I'm going to find a way to make this work. I'll find a way to get him. You'll see. After all this, she probably don't want him anyway."

"Nope. I still like my plan better. Kill the baby. Her too if we have too. And let's just forget this. We should've just tried to open something with the money that we had left or something. This was a bad idea. Let's just fix it and go."

"I'm trying to fix it now."

"NO! Getting rid of the baby is the only way that it will be fixed. You want the baby. I don't."

I shook my head.

"Let's just go," she begged.

I wanted to. Hell, we didn't even have to go through the divorce dance since in reality, Strawberry wasn't really married. Fuck the money too. We still had some. But no matter how I tried to spin it, I just didn't want to leave my son behind.

"I got this. I promise you. I got this."

She continued to rant and rave, but I knew how to shut her up. I knew exactly what she needed. She pointed her finger at me and I ignored her and started to pull down her panties.

"Move! Move! Where is she huh? Where is that bitch and that baby? Just let me kick her ass. I'll show you how to get rid of a baby! Just let me kick her in the stomach a few times. She's not having your baby! Where is she? Then we can just go. Let's just go!"

In a hurry to calm her down, I tugged on the sides of her cranberry colored thong, and I threw the ripped lace over my head.

"Move. Don't touch me!"

"Oh, I can't touch you, now? You belong to me, remember? Everything on you belongs to me. You are my wife. Always remember that," I said to her and before she could say anything else, I grabbed her mouth and kissed her.

She resisted for a while longer, but I knew that eventually she was going to submit and allow me to please her. She did. I punished her with pounds of pleasure and frustration for about an hour. Once I heard her start to snore, I got up.

I tip-toed around the small apartment. It was nothing like the big, beautiful house that we'd been renting. After Strawberry drove by that night, and saw the lights on and heard the music, we knew that we would have to go. She was being too nosey. I watched her from the window. Of course I was there that night. There was never a job, or a conference. I had been there with Fran…my real wife. But then Strawberry shows up. Right then I knew that she might be a problem, but it was my choice to keep going. Fran suggested that we find someone else or just scrap the whole plan. But I kept going.

I looked back at my sleeping beauty. I'd never loved anyone the way that I love her. My love for her was real.

I knew that she was going to be pissed when she woke up to find that I wasn't there. But I had to go see about Strawberry and my son.

I shut the door and headed almost an hour away.

"What you gonna do man? What you gonna do?"

I talked to myself as I drove. Either way, somebody was gonna get hurt; or end up dead.

Fran was so jealous of Strawberry and the fact that she was carrying my baby. All she did was bitch about it. If she wasn't cussing, she was fussing. If she wasn't screaming about it, she was crying over it. Damn. I didn't mean to hurt her. I was always careful but I messed up. Even once I got the woman to marry me, I would deal her some story about wanting to wait until the time was right to have kids, so I would get her to take the pill or something. But I slipped up. And now I had to figure out how to fix it.

Memories of the day that my son died crossed my mind. I remembered the last time that I saw him smile. I also remembered the sight of his little arm coming out of the water. I miss him. Two years wasn't long enough. I'd needed more time with him. I thought about how we just buried his body by the lake and disappeared. No one knew he was there. We didn't have a funeral. We didn't even tell the authorities. We just buried him and left. He would've been turning ten, the same month that Strawberry was due. My son with her wouldn't replace him. But a part of me felt like I needed him. I needed this second chance.

I was no fool. Of course Strawberry wasn't just going to hand over the baby. I'm going to have to take him from her. But for now, I was just trying to keep her away from Fran's wrath; keep her and the baby alive.

Finally arriving at the hotel that I'd stashed Strawberry in, I used the key that I'd hid inside my wallet and entered the room. I looked around but there was no need.

Strawberry was gone.

****

Chapter THREE

"Thank you for coming to get me Ray," I said to him.

He'd finally called me back. I told him where I was and he came running.

"No problem. What were you doing at the hotel anyway?"

"It's a long story."

"I've got time. Or let me guess, it has something to do with Tobias?"

I nodded.

"So, I was right. He is hiding something?"

"Yeah, a whole damn wife."

Ray took his eyes off of the road and looked at me.

"What?"

"Yep. I can't go home Ray."

"You can stay at my place until you figure things out."

"Uh, I don't want to intrude."

"On what? On who? There's no one there but me. As I told you, she and I are over. And you and I are just friends. I'm helping out a friend."

He drove and I smiled at him. I was actually happy that he offered. I knew that I would be safe with him, well, whenever he was home that is.

"Thank you Ray. I appreciate it."

"No problem."

Ray was quiet, but there was something about his silence. It was as though he wanted to say something, but he didn't know how to say it.

"How is Shelly?"

"I don't know. I haven't been back to the hospital. Last I talked to April, she was still the same." Thinking of her, I started to cry and Ray rubbed my shoulder.

This was all too much. I was pregnant, emotional and I felt like I was losing my mind.

My sister was fighting for her life and my "husband" has a wife. And the bitch was trying to kill me!

It's just too much.

I called April to check on Shelly again and she and Mama wanted to know where I was. I told them to keep Brian away from her. But they feared that she wasn't going to make it. I wanted to be there. I really needed to be there.

But seeing Tobias's name and number pop up on my cell phone, I knew that it was best that I stayed away. At least until I could figure out my next move.

Taking a pen out of my purse and after writing down Mama, April's and Ray's phone numbers on a piece of paper, I tossed my cell phone out of the window.

"Okay, Strawberry, what's really going on? I can't help you if you don't tell me everything."

"Nothing. I'll be fine. I just need a little time," was all I said, but the way that he grunted, I knew that he didn't believe me. After driving for a little while longer, we pulled up at a townhouse. It was gorgeous but I couldn't help but notice that it was only about three minutes away from my house.

"This is home."

"You've lived here the whole time?" Since you moved out?" I never knew where he lived; it was really none of my business. But I hadn't known that he'd lived right around the corner from me, all of this time.

"Yes. I was never too far away."

I guess in a way it was kind of cute. After all, he'd confessed to me that he'd never stopped loving me and that letting me go was a mistake. Maybe it was. Maybe divorcing him was a mistake. Marrying Tobias sure as hell was.

"There isn't going to be any issues right? Your wife…"

"Ex-wife, times two," he smirked.

"Ex-wife, isn't going to pop up or anything is she? I can't handle anymore "wife" drama."

"No. Everything is fine. She and I are over. For Good. Forever."

He led me inside and I smiled. It was clean. And it smelled good too. He'd definitely had some help decorating. The whole place just had a woman's touch to it.

"Make yourself at home. I have an extra bedroom. You can use that one. I have to get back to work. Do you think you will be okay until I get back?"

I nodded and as he turned around to leave, I grabbed his hand.

"Thank you Ray," I said and he hugged me and kissed my cheek.

"Anytime. Anything."

I watched him from the window as he raced down the street in his patrol car. I should've never let him go. After glancing to make sure that the front door was locked, I headed to look around.

Though there were decorative pictures all over the walls, there were none of him and the woman that he'd married not too long ago. As a matter of fact, there wasn't a trace of her anywhere. I looked in his room, in his drawers, closets, under his bathroom sink; nothing.

It seemed as though he'd been there all alone for quite some time. But I remembered her answering his phone, that night that I got drunk, so I knew that she had been around at some time or another. But one would have easily thought that Ray's recent ex-wife…didn't exist.

~***~

"She's awake," Mama said.

I jumped up from the couch. Shelly was awake.

"I'm on my way." I hung up, and called a taxi on Ray's house phone. I had been hiding at his place for three straight days. I hadn't been home. I hadn't tried to go get my car or any of my clothes. I hadn't even stepped outside to catch a nice breeze. But there was no way in the hell that I wasn't going to go to the hospital to see my sister.

At that moment I didn't care about Tobias, or his hidden wife, or anything else. I just cared about Shelly.

A little while later, in one of Ray's t-shirts and a pair of his gym shorts, I arrived at the hospital and immediately I spotted Tobias's car. He was sitting inside of it, facing the hospital entrance, as though he was waiting around to see if I would show up. There was nowhere to hide, so I simply got out of the taxi and wobbled as fast as I could inside of the hospital. I kept looking behind me to see if he was following me but he wasn't.

"Where is she?" I asked as soon as I got off of the elevator.

"She still isn't doing too good but at least she's awake."

"Is she breathing on her own?"

"No."

I hugged and kissed my Mama and baby sister.

"Okay, when can we go back?"

"We've already been. Brian is back there now."

The sound of his name made my skin crawl. I didn't trust him alone with her. Who knows, he was probably responsible for this.

A few minutes later, he appeared and I stared at him. He looked at me as though he already knew that I knew the truth about him.

"How could you?"

He just looked at me.

"You knew what Tobias was up to. How could you?"

"It wasn't my place or my business," he said.

"Oh, but I know some of your business that I'm sure my sister is going to love to hear," I scowled him.

"Strawberry, what are you talking about?"

"This low-life bastard is probably the reason that Shelly is in here fighting for her life right now! He isn't who he says that he is. He's dirty. He ruined my life for a quick buck. And he has been lying to Shelly."

Mama looked at him, as he stared at me.

"This isn't the time or place Strawberry."

"Yeah. This isn't the time. Or the place," Brian said in a low, cold tone, as though he was trying to threaten me but I stuck my middle finger up at him to assure him that I wasn't scared of him.

I turned my back to him and headed to see my sister; alone. I looked at her. She wasn't moving, she wasn't doing anything. She looked so pale and nothing like her usual, diva-self. I felt overwhelmed with sadness, but I held back my tears as her eyes looked in my direction.

"Hey, can you hear me?"

She didn't nod or do anything. She just looked at me.

"Girl, you look a mess," I joked with her but of course she didn't give me a response.

Touching her hand, she attempted to squeeze my finger.

"I love you Shelly. You are going to get through this."

I couldn't hold back the tears any longer. I hated seeing her so helpless. I needed her. She would know what to do about Tobias and his other wife. April's non-verbal ass sure as hell wouldn't be of any help.

After another minute or so, I let go of her hand.

"Shelly, do you know who did this to you?"

At first, she just laid there and then…

She nodded.

"You do? You know who did this?"

She nodded again. But before I could ask her anything else, she closed her eyes.

~***~

Tobias rode by Ray's house again.

I knew that it was only a matter of time before he'd figured out where I was. This was the fifth time that I'd caught him riding by, and I knew that he was looking for me.

I had gotten another cell phone, with a new number and of course I didn't bother giving the number to him but he'd sent me more than a few e-mails. He'd stated that I was safe, and that I didn't have to worry about his wife anymore. He also said that for my sake, he would sign divorce papers. And of course he mentioned the baby. He even had the nerve to say that he was sorry for everything. But sorry wasn't good enough.

"What are you looking at out there?" Ray asked.

I still hadn't told him everything. Only that I knew that Tobias was lying about who he really was, and that somehow he was married to someone else too. Ray had always been a stand-up cop, but here lately, I was wondering if he would get dirty; just for me. He would look up stuff or do little things like that, but I wanted to know if he would be willing to do anything else. Something that only he and I could know. But I knew that he was going to need a little motivation.

"Nothing."

I walked over to Ray. He had been more than generous. Words couldn't express how much I appreciated what he was doing for me. But I couldn't help but wonder what else he might be willing to do for little ole' me.

"Did you move all of your money?"

"Yes. Half to my secret savings and I put the other half in April's account."

Surprisingly, Tobias hadn't tried to clear out the joint account. I'd seen a few transactions, but for the most part, he hadn't tried to move any big amounts of money. But I did. Every cent that was mine, was gone. He had better be glad that I left what little was his. I should've taken it all. He wouldn't have had a problem doing it to me.

"I need to go see my lawyer about the divorce. Or is that even necessary, since he isn't really who he says that he is? I mean, are we really even married? I mean, technically, I'm married to someone that doesn't exist…right? He told me that Tobias isn't his real name and that Brian helped him change his identity."

"Brian?"

"Yep."

Ray didn't say anything. He just shook his head.

I sat next to him and he stared at me.

"What?"

"Nothing. Not to get off topic but you're just so beautiful."

"Stop lying. Have you seen this double chin? If it gets any bigger, I'm going to start making it pay rent. I've gained over fifty pounds and I look like I swallowed a midget." I was getting bigger and bigger every day and I still had a little while to go.

Ray laughed, and touched my face.

"And you're still beautiful. You've always been beautiful to me. Your eyes. Your smile. You're the prettiest girl in the world," Ray said.

I stared at him. I found myself wondering why I'd ever let him go. We grew apart, but we hadn't had any real big issues. At the moment, all of our problems seemed so small compared to what I was going through with Tobias.

"Everything is going to be okay," he said.

I smiled at him.

"I'm not so sure."

"They will be."

My emotions were all over the place and my hormones were raging. It was weird. I wanted to cry and screw, all at the same time. "Kiss me Ray."

He looked at me as though he was unsure.

"Kiss me."

"Strawberry, I don't know if---," I didn't wait for him to finish his sentence. I leaned in and kissed him instead. He kissed me back instantly but after only a second or two, he stopped, cleared his throat and then he stood up.

"Where are you going?"

"Um, to take a nap. I have to work tonight."

"Can I come too?"

I could tell that he was uncomfortable. Obviously he still saw me as somebody else's wife. Well, of course he did. And I was sure that my pregnant belly was even more of a reminder.

"Sure,"

I'd been in his bedroom a few times, while he was at work, being nosey, but I hadn't been in his bed. He climbed in and patted the space next to him, for me to join him. I did and we made ourselves comfortable.

"I don't know what to do."

"Don't worry about it."

Ray wrapped his arms around me and I felt a small flicking type of feeling in my clitoris. I hadn't been held in a long while, and to be honest, being in his arms felt good.

I inhaled the scent of his skin and I snuggled close to him. I was hoping that he tried to be a pervert but he didn't.

Ray fell asleep and soon after so did I.

Hours later, he woke me up to tell me that he was headed to his late shift. I rolled over in his bed and laid for a little while longer. Just as I started to doze off, the alarm clock beside his bed sounded, scaring the hell out of me. He was already up and gone. Had he waited on the alarm, he would have been late! I hurriedly smacked it, accidently knocking it off of the small table.

Wiping my eyes, I leaned over to get it, but something shiny caught my eye. I picked it up. It was a charm; for a bracelet. It was of a dolphin, with clear and blue diamonds in the center. I flipped it over and read the initials.

I recognized it. I'd bought it…

For my little sister April.

So, what was it doing here?

****

Chapter FOUR

I stared at Tobias as he walked into the doctor's office. I had an appointment to check on the baby, and I had rescheduled twice already. I couldn't miss this one.

Just like I figured, Tobias showed up on the scene. I was convinced that somehow he'd shoved a tracking device up my ass or something.

"Mrs. Fields? We're ready for you."

Tobias walked hastily towards me.

"Please. I don't want my husband to go back with me," I stated just as Tobias reached us.

Tobias didn't say anything.

"He's following me. We're separated. He beats me. Oh, he beats me so bad. That's why I had to reschedule. He gave me a black eye last week and I had to wait for it to heal. Can you still see the mark, just a little? Please. I'm afraid for my life. I think my baby's life is in danger. Please make him leave. Please."

The doctor looked at me concerned. Tobias looked at me as though he wanted to snap my neck

Speaking of necks, his was all scratched up as though he'd been in a fight, with a woman. The scratches were visible which in my opinion made my lie even more believable, since there was clear evidence of some kind of struggle.

"I'm sorry. I can't let you back there Mr. Fields. I'm going to have to ask you to leave."

Tobias seemed to be in deep thought but he didn't put up a fight. He just turned around and walked away.

I could tell that he was mad. He was so heated that the Devil himself might make a U-turn before coming his way today. But I didn't care. He was about to see a whole new side of me. The old side of me; the side of me that was willing to do anything to get what I wanted. The side of me that was determined to get through this; on top. And most importantly alive.

Once he walked out the door, I turned to face the doctor.

"He has such a bad temper. He has a terrible drinking problem and he's so abusive. I can't allow him around my son. How do I go about getting sole custody?" I said as we headed to the back. I smiled as I thought of one small fact. I'd just made my first allegation about Tobias to my doctor. I'd voiced this so-called abuse. I'd gone on record and said it and Tobias hadn't even tried to deny it. Shooting Tobias and getting away with it, might be easier than I thought after all. Now this is how you get away with murder.

~***~

I stared at my little sister's wrist. Her charm bracelet made noises as she moved her hand around in a circle as Mama talked to her. She wasn't saying much, as always, but she was listening.

I studied the charms. I'd purchased the bracelet as a high school graduation present. Every milestone, or whenever I'm just feeling proud of her, I purchase her another charm.

The dolphin charm was missing.

"April? Where is your dolphin charm?"

April glanced down at her wrist. I had the charm in my purse. I hadn't mentioned my finding to Ray as of yet. I wanted to say something to her first.

"I don't know. Just noticed that it was missing."

"When was the last time that you saw it?"

"I'm not sure. It's probably at home."

"If it's not at home, where else would it be?"

She shrugged but didn't respond.

Hmm…

April wouldn't have sex with my ex-husband right? Hell, Ray wouldn't have sex with her, I think. From what he said, and what he showed, he was still in love with me. I'd still been staying at his house and he was taking real, good care of me; in so many ways. We've gotten physical. He still wouldn't have, quote on quote, "sex" with me. But he was eating "my box", every night. I told him that I was horny and I guess that was the only way that he was willing to oblige. I guess I would feel funny about humping a pregnant lady too. But we had been getting really close. He was constantly telling me that he loved me. He was constantly telling me that I was beautiful and that he wished that we could just start over. I believed him. I really believed him. But, what about the charm?

We were sitting around at the hospital. Shelly had just had another surgery. There were parts of a bullet stuck inside of her, and a few important organs had been injured by the others. She was in a medical induce coma at the moment, and hadn't been awake since the last time that I saw her. I wished she could have told me who had done this to her. But I was sure that the man sitting across from me already knew.

Brian.

"So why did you marry Shelly?"

"Because I love her."

"And what else?"

"That's it."

"Surely that isn't it. We both know that Tobias married me for my money, with your help, so why did you marry her?" Immediately Mama started to ask me questions about my statement, but I ignored her and waited on Brian's response.

"I'm not like your "husband". Like I said, I married her because I love her. Check me out. She's the only wife that I have. And the only one that I need. Mr. "Tobias" as you call him, is just a little greedy. Wouldn't you agree?"

Brian taunted me. It was almost as if he found it funny or something.

"Why did you try to break into my house? Shelly found the mask."

"I didn't try to break-in. Believe me if I wanted in, I would've gotten in. I was asked to do a favor, and I did it."

"A favor. What? Scare me?"

"Something like that. Fear causes people to think unclearly. Most of the time, it's meant to serve a purpose. Like that little mugging."

"You? You were responsible for the mugging?"

"What mugging?" Mama asked.

"Shake you up a little bit. And then Tobias called right on time. It gave you a sense of comfort. Dependency on him. Just like the break-in before Mama's birthday party.

Fear made you want him around you all the time. It made it easier for him to get close. Easier to get you exactly where he wanted you."

Mama was fussing at Brian. She was getting upset and cursing, and April stood her up and led her away. Of course she didn't have much to say, but I could see on her face that what Brian was saying to me, made her angry.

"How dare you! You've been a part of our family for years! Didn't that mean anything to you? You knew that Tobias didn't love me. Would it have killed you to say something?"

"No. It wouldn't have killed me. But we both know that I wouldn't have gotten paid if I had. Now would I?"

I wanted to slapped the hell out of him.

"I can't wait to tell her what kind of man she married."

"Trust me. She already knows."

"Not the truth. Not the truth about you."

"That's where you're wrong. She does."

"So she knows about all of this? About your mother? And that you were paid to change Tobias's identity, so that he could seduce me and steal from me?"

"Like I said. She already knows," he said and then he got up and walked away.

I didn't believe him.

Shelly would have told me. Hell, she'd told me everything else and she was about to tell me more the day that she was shot. He was lying. He was playing with my head. He was trying to make her out to be something that she wasn't; something like him. I knew her. She's my sister. She would have told me. She was trying to tell me before she was shot.

I sat there, thinking about everything that he'd said. Tobias had really played me. Everything was planned. Everything was a part of one big, stupid ass plan! My feelings were hurt, but I still refused to cry. The more I thought about how everything played out, the more I wanted to do something crazy. Something to get even. And I knew just what I was going to do to.

~***~

"How in the hell did you get my number?"

"Brian." I didn't even bother to ask how Brian had gotten it. Who knows!

"We need to talk Strawberry."

"No. We don't. The only talking we need to do is to a lawyer. I don't have anything to say to you Tobias. I'm done. It's over."

"I've already filed for the divorce."

"When?"

"A few days ago. You don't really need it since you aren't really married to the real me. But for legally reason, for you, I filed for it to make it official with the courts. Just in case you ever wanted to get married again."

I was never getting married again! And I mean never!

"Good. Then we really don't have anything else to talk about." I didn't want to talk to him. What was there to say? Hey, how's your other wife today? Let's all go on a date. Better yet, let's all move into one big ass house, together, and live happily-ever after. Hell, knowing them, they might not object to that. She allowed him to screw other women any damn way.

"We have a child to talk about Tiffany. And I know that you took all of the money out of the account. I let you. I don't want your money. I don't want anything from you. I just want to be there for my son."

"No."

"What do you mean no?"

"No. He's my son. Go have a baby with your real wife. We don't need you. Just go away."

"I've lost one son already. I won't lose another one."

"I said no. I'm going to make sure that you or your crazy bitch, don't come anywhere near him!"

Tobias chuckled in a scary sort of way.

"Tiffany, I'm not going anywhere; at least not without my son. You want me out of your life for good? The only way that's going to happen is if you gave him to me because other than that, I'm not going anywhere. Now, I gave you your divorce. I gave you your money. But I'm not giving you my son. You don't want to see me pissed off Tiffany. If you think I'm married to a crazy bitch, then you ain't seen nothing yet. Word of advice: don't try to keep my son away from me."

And with that, he hung up before I could reply.

"Everything okay?" Ray asked.

"He filed for a divorce."

"That's good, right?"

"Yeah. But for some reason it doesn't seem like enough."

Ray just looked at me.

"Maybe once the divorce is final, he will just go away."

"I don't think so," I said rubbing my stomach.

Tobias's words played over and over again in my head. Yep. I was going to have to kill him. And I was going to get Ray to help me get away with it.

Ray's phone started to ring and he looked at it. And then looked at me with a smile.

"So, what's next? After the divorce? If you want to stay here with me until you are sure about what you want to do, with the house or until you feel safe, you can. Who knows, maybe all of what's going on, happened for a reason. Not that what he did to you is okay. It's not. But our relationship, is better than ever. I feel like the connection between us is even stronger than it was when we were married."

I looked at Ray. Why in the world did he seem to love me so much? After all of these years? After I'd turned him down and married another man right in his face? I would've said to hell with me, if I was him. But he was right here.

"Can I ask you something?"

"Anything."

"Were you ever really remarried Ray? I mean, I've been a little nosey and I haven't seen anything about this other so-called wife that you had for a few months. No pictures. No divorce papers, unless you keep them in your car or something. But they aren't anywhere around here. They aren't where you keep ours. So did you ever really get remarried? I mean, or were you just trying to make me jealous?"

"What? No Strawberry, I was remarried. It just didn't work out."

"To who? Why is there nothing about her in your house? What was her name? You never even mention her." I'd never known Ray to lie about anything, but Tobias had me looking at everyone in a different light. And as I said, I'd found it strange that there was nothing about her in his house.

"I was married to Delilah Phillips."

Wait…what?

Delilah Phillips? The woman whose fingerprint was on my clutch? Huh?

"I was married to Delilah Phillips. Yes, the same one whose fingerprint was found on your clutch. I confronted her about that. She told me that she followed you to the club that night. She told me that she'd tried to get your attention and ask you some questions about our relationship. She said she reached out to tap you but you were hurrying out the door."

I remembered Shelly saying that a woman had asked her where I'd gone that night at the club. She said that she'd called me by name. Maybe that was her. I remembered the night that I'd called Ray's phone. She'd called me by name then too.

"She knew that I'd come over to your house the day before we got married. I told her that we talked and that I just wanted to close that chapter. But she wasn't convinced. She felt like I still loved you. But she married me anyway. I guess she spotted you in the club that night and wanted to ask a few questions for herself. She knew who you were. I'd shown her plenty of pictures of you."

"Why did you ask me if I knew her?"

"I just asked. I'd already told you that we'd found a print, so when it came back hers, I told you the truth. I didn't want to lie about it."

Something didn't seem right to me. Something that he was saying sounded fishy.

"She was at your wedding."

"Who?"

"Delilah."

I looked at him confused.

"She and I had decided to go our separate ways by then. But she blamed you. She blamed the love that I have for you. Though I was still in love with you, I told her that I wasn't and told her that you were getting married to someone else. I have no idea how she knew where your wedding was going to be but she called me and told me that she was there. She told me that I'd been telling the truth and that she was watching you, at that moment, with your new husband. But strangely afterwards, she'd said that the divorce was the best thing for us to do. She wanted to go through with it. She said that I'd never looked at her the way that he was looking at you and she said that she deserved that."

She was at my wedding. Suddenly I remembered the woman dressed like one of the workers that kept staring at me. That had to be her. That had to be Delilah Phillips.

I couldn't explain it, but it seemed as though an eerie type of feeling had entered the room. But since I had Ray talking, I decided to keep with my questions.

"Ray, why was April's charm beside your bed?"

He looked at me confused. I showed him what I was talking about.

"I've never seen that before."

"It was beside your bed. What was it doing there? Why was my sister's charm in your bedroom?"

"I don't know Strawberry. I'm telling you. I've never see that before."

"Then how did it get there?"

"I don't know but I didn't put it there and April damn sure didn't bring it here. Wait. You don't think that I would ever have something going on with your sister, do you?"

"I don't know what to think."

Ray looked at me concerned.

"I love you too much to do something like that to you."

"Yeah, I thought that about Tobias too."

"Don't ever compare me to him. Ever. I don't know where the charm came from. Maybe it was Delilah's. She loved jewelry. Maybe it just looks like the one that April has."

I turned the charm over.

"No. I had all of hers engraved. It has April's initials on it."

He looked closely at the charm and then shrugged his shoulders.

"I don't know how it got there Strawberry," he said. And then he offered to go get us something to eat. He headed out and I was left to dwell on my thoughts. I was starting to wonder if being there was such a good idea.

April's charm didn't just walk into his house. Something was wrong here. Something was very wrong.

One of them, both of them, was lying to me. But why? What were they hiding? Why was everybody lying to me!

My phone started to ring and I saw that it was Tobias. I ignored it and then there came a knock on the front door.

"Open the door Tiffany," Tobias said.

"Go away or I'll call Ray. He should be back any minute."

I heard him chuckle. And then he started to kick the front door. Literally.

"Open the door!"

"No! I'm calling Ray!"

"Go ahead. Call Ray. But just so you know, hell, you're safer with me then you are with him anyway."

What? What the hell does that mean?

He continued to kick the door and instead of calling Ray, I headed to open it.

"What did you mean by that?" I screamed as soon as Tobias and I were face to face.

He immediately looked at my stomach and then back at me.

"He's obsessed with you Strawberry. And obsession is a very dangerous thing," Tobias said, and stepping into Ray's house, as though I'd invited him in.

"He's not obsessed me."

"Oh yes, he is."

"How? And how would you know that?" I asked him as if I could take his word on anything.

"Trust me. I know. You don't have to believe me. Now. But one day you will. I don't want you here. You don't have to be here. You can go home. No one is going to bother you."

"Yea. Right."

"She's not going to bother you."

I rolled my eyes. As far as I was concerned, a bitch that comes to your house with a chainsaw, will do anything!

"You may hate me. You may think that I don't give a damn about you. But one thing that you can be sure of is that I care about that little boy in your belly. Take my advice. Don't stay here. Go home. I hope you ain't been over here giving him that pregnant pussy or you really gonna' have a problem on your hands. Go home Tiffany."

He turned to walk away. Just as he got into his car, the white Mercedes stopped and waited for him to pull off. The windows were tinted, so I couldn't see her face, but the real Mrs. Fields was yet again on the scene. She drove off behind him, and I shut Ray's front door.

I read the incoming text message that Tobias sent to my phone.

"I got her. Don't worry about her. Just go home."

After reading it, and thinking for a second about Tobias, his wife, Ray, April, and Delilah Phillips, I didn't respond to Tobias. I texted Ray instead. I asked him where he was and then I told him that when he got back, I was going home.

~***~

"Have you and Ray had sex?" I asked my little sister April.

"What?"

"You heard me. Have you and Ray had sex?"

"Have you?" she asked.

"Don't be a smart ass. Answer my question."

"No."

"Your charm, the missing dolphin one was at his house, beside his bed. So, April, are you sleeping with my ex-husband?"

"No." I waited for her to say more but of course she didn't. She never did.

"You can tell me. I won't be mad," I lied. Of course I would be livid and probably smack the taste out of her mouth but she shook her head.

"No."

"Tell me the truth."

"About what?"

"Tell me if you had sex with Ray."

She gave me a blank stare. She just sat there. Unbothered.

"Damn it! This isn't the time for you to act like your usual weird, nonchalant-self April! Open your damn mouth and tell me why your charm, that I bought you, was beside my ex-husband's bed!"

She shrugged. "I don't know. If I fucked him, I would tell you," she said rudely. "Like I said, how it got there, I don't know."

"You don't know? Somebody knows something! You're lying to me. He's lying to me too. What? Do I look stupid to you?"

"Is that a trick question? You're stupid if you think I would sleep with Ray. You're my sister."

I stared at her. She barely gave me eye contact. But she didn't really seem nervous. Hell she didn't really seem to care about what I was saying to her.

"Then how did it get there? If you weren't in his bed, his bedroom, his house, how did it get there?"

She shrugged. "I don't know."

In frustration, I threw my phone at her. I started yelling but she didn't say anything.

"Bitch if I wasn't pregnant, I would choke you until you told me the truth!" April didn't say anything. She allowed my phone to drop to the floor as she stood up, grabbed her purse and walked out the front door.

"I'll never forgive you if you slept with him!" I screamed after her, but she didn't say anything.

I screamed at the top of my lungs.

I had so many questions, and not enough answers and I was starting to realize that maybe I hadn't just been sleeping with the enemy; apparently everyone else around me was my enemy too.

Tobias called again. I didn't answer it.

I was back home. And so far, everything had been fine. No issues. Tobias's wife hadn't shown up. He hadn't popped up to harass me. Everything had been going fine.

I had an upgraded alarm system. A gun. Bars installed on all of the windows. The front door fixed and a few extra locks added to it. I even bought a damn dog.

So, for the most part, I felt safe. By the time anybody made it through all of the other mess, the police would be on their way and I would be waiting for them, gun in hand; finger on the trigger.

Tobias had gotten all of his things out of the house before I'd even gotten there. We were set to sign the papers the day after tomorrow and for the most part, I just wanted it all to be over.

I locked up the house and watched April sit for a while in my driveway. I wondered if accusing her was too much.

She was already a little different and being that no one really knew how her mind worked, I didn't want her to do something irrational; especially if she was telling the truth. I remembered that her and Shelly had gotten into an argument once and she shut down on everyone for weeks. She didn't call, come around or anything. I had to go catch her in class just to make sure that she wasn't dead. In my thoughts, I vowed to call her and apologize the next morning. Maybe I was a little out of line.

I just wanted to know the truth. I felt like everyone was lying to me and I just wanted to know the truth.

I headed towards the nursery.

Tobias had added to it while I was away. He'd painted and placed fun, vibrant wall decals all over the place. Glow in the dark stars on the ceiling. It really was a room fit for a little prince. Too bad he wasn't going to get to see him enjoy it.

I was still serious about getting rid of Tobias. I was trying to figure out how I was going to do it. Telling him that he wasn't going to get to be around the baby already made him angry, so I knew that one day, I was going to start an argument, and hopefully everything would go from there. He was going to have to come over to the house at some point for it to work. A set up, just liked I'd done with

Jake Dawson. Only this time, he was going to be leaving in a body bag, instead of in handcuffs.

Then I would be waiting on his wife. I would tell the police all that I knew about their little scam and then when she came for me, I would be waiting for her too. I guess it would help if I at least knew what she looked like.

Leaving the baby's room, I called to check of Shelly. These days, she had been improving. Doctors said that she was expected to make a full recovery. I couldn't wait for her to get better. I had a few questions that I wanted to ask her too. I wanted to know if Brian was telling the truth. I wanted to know if she had known as much as he said that she did.

I made my way back to the living room and made myself comfortable on the couch. My gun was on the coffee table and my new dog, Killer, was right next to me.

At about six months pregnant now, I was tired. Pregnancy was no joke. I was sure that I would never get pregnant again.

I closed my eyes and I tried to get some sleep. And for a while I did. Until I jumped up an hour or so later in a cold, disturbing sweat.

It was another nightmare. But this time, it wasn't about Jake Dawson, or someone trying to come after me to avenge his death; it was about Tobias's nameless, faceless, hidden wife. I dreamt that a faceless woman was standing over me with a knife, preparing to cut my baby out of my stomach.

I looked around the room. The dog sat looking at me. I'd gotten him from a dog adoption agency. He used to have a blind owner, until he passed away, so they vowed that he was smart, and very overprotective. I could tell. He waited for me to calm down and lay back down. He laid his head on his paws, but he never took his eyes off of me.

Suddenly, his ears stood straight up and he started to growl. I looked towards the patio doors as he stood up. I didn't see a shadow or anything but he continued to growl and head towards it, so I followed.

I peeked through the blinds, but I didn't see anyone. But he continued to growl, assuring me that someone was there. I was sure that they couldn't get in; at least not easily. I'd did some upgrades to that door as well. But I still wanted to know who was out there.

Suddenly, Killer started to bark and after looking at him for a second, I turned my attention back outside.

The figure caught me by surprise, and I jumped. I could see them. Whoever it was. I couldn't tell if it was a man or a woman. But it wasn't like I even had to guess. I was sure that it was her. Tobias's real wife.

Killer continued to bark and I went to grab the gun off of the coffee table. I wondered why the alarm hadn't sounded. I made it back to the patio door, but when I looked outside, whoever it was, was gone.

I grabbed my phone and called Tobias.

"You had better tell your "wife" to stay the hell away from my house! I swear if she comes here again, I'm going to shoot her. And trust me, I won't miss!" I yelled at Tobias.

"What? What are you talking about Tiffany? She isn't at your house."

"What? Yes, she is! Don't lie to me! I just saw her."

"No. You didn't. I'm looking right at her. She's asleep," he said. Tobias took the phone closer to her so that I could hear her snoring.

What? Well, if it wasn't her, who in the hell was it then?

****

Chapter FIVE

"And there you have it. You are officially divorced."

The lawyer smiled as though he was happy to be divorcing yet another couple, but technically we were never really married in the first place.

Tobias stood up and he reached out his hand to help me up but I rolled my eyes at it and stood up on my own.

We didn't speak as we walked out of the office and headed for our cars.

"How are you feeling?"

"I'm fine."

"Can I feel him?" Tobias asked. I didn't even answer him.

"So that really wasn't her at the house the other night?"

"No."

Hmm…It was someone. I'd seen them. I'm sure that they were there.

"Let me stay with you until you have the baby."

"Uh. No. You've caused enough problems in my life already."

"I want to make sure that you're safe."

"You've used that line before remember?"

"But it's different now. You're carrying my child Strawberry. I won't let anyone hurt you. Not her. Not anyone. Hell somebody is creeping around your house, and I know for a fact that it wasn't her. She was with me."

I looked into his eyes. The crazy thing was that I actually believe him.

"I will protect you. Like I told you. I don't want your money, anymore, or anything from you. I just want to make sure that you're safe. And that the baby is safe. That's it."

I shook my head no.

I got into my car but Tobias grabbed the door.

"My real name is Darren." Tobias said and then he let go of my door and walked away.

Darren? He didn't look like a Darren.

I watched him drive away.

I sat there for a moment. I stared at the divorce papers. I remembered how I'd felt the first time, but this time I felt different. I didn't feel so empty. I actually felt relieved. At least this part was done and over with.

Tobias started to call me and when I answered he asked if I was okay and he wanted to know why I was still sitting there. Rolling my eyes, I put my car in reverse.

But a car stopped me from going anywhere.

I stared at the white Mercedes in my rearview mirror.

Just the lady I've been dying to see.

The car just sat there. I beeped my horn, but the car didn't move. I waited to see if she was going to get out of the car, but she didn't. So I did.

I was tired of this. I wanted to see her face and I wanted to know what kind of woman would allow her husband screw and marry other women. To be honest, I might just punch the hell out of her. Maybe it would knock some sense into her!

I walked right up to her car and knocked on her window. I couldn't see inside of the car at all. I knocked on the window again and waited.

My stomach growled and I touched my stomach. Just as I did, the window rolled down, just an inch, and she flicked the butt of a lit cigarette in my face.

Bitch!

Before I could react, she rolled back up the window.

I punched the window, hard, but the glass didn't break.

"What, you scared? Get the hell out of the car bitch!" I kicked at her car, and grabbed on the door handle, but she just sat there. She didn't get out and she didn't roll the window back down so that I could see her. Once a crowd started to form, finally, she drove away.

I watched the car until it was out of sight.

Bitch, this means war!

~***~

"Why are you in my driveway?" I asked Tobias, or maybe I should call him Darren. He still answered to Tobias so I would stick with that.

"I told you. I won't let anything happen to you. So I'm going to sleep out here in the car."

"Go home. Tell your wife to come out here and sleep in the car. I got something for her ass. Call her and tell her to come on by," I taunted him. I was still pissed at her for throwing the cigarette in my face. I had a burn mark on my nose, and I wasn't going to satisfied until I got my lick back.

"Just go home. I'm fine."

"Nah, I'll just sleep here," he said and then he hung up the phone. I looked out the window for a little while longer. I knew that before long, his wife was going to show up and I was hoping that she would. I texted him and told him to leave again, but he only refused.

Fine. Sleep in the car then.

I headed to my bedroom. Just as I got comfortable, my phone started to ring. It was Ray. We hadn't talked much lately. He'd called, but I ignored him. I still didn't know what was going on with him and April. So, I kept my distance. And with Tobias's comments, I really didn't know what to think of it all. I hadn't heard from April and I hadn't made it around to apologizing to her for my behavior. I needed to.

"I've been calling you, but I haven't been able to reach you. How are you? Why did you leave? I told you that you could stay for as long as you needed to. I was actually enjoying your company."

I wanted to bring up the charm again, but I decided not to.

"Thanks, but I'm fine. Hey, let me call you back. My other line is beeping."

I pulled the phone away from my ear and saw that it was a number that I didn't recognize.

"Hello?"

"Is my husband over there bitch?"

I looked at the number again. It wasn't private anything. Good. I guess I was going to have to be nice to Ray so I could get him to trace it for me.

I smirked and decided that I wanted to be petty.

"Well, actually…he is. Why don't you come on over here and get him?" I said and eagerly awaited her response.

I tried to see if I recognized her voice but she talked low and with so much attitude that it almost sounded animated.

"Trust me, you don't want me to come over there."

"Oh. But I do. Please do," I said to her.

"What kind of woman has a baby by someone else's husband?"

"I guess I'm the same kind of woman that pimps out her husband's penis for profit. Selling your own ass would've been easier. And newsflash, I thought that he was my husband."

"But he isn't. He's mine."

"You can have him. But word on the street is, he liked getting it from me just a little bit better. He said your *cookie* was old, and overused. Hmm, I might give him a little taste. Just to show him what he's been missing. You coming over yet?" I said to her intentionally pushing her buttons. She didn't respond. She just hung up. I laughed and waited a while before heading back to see if Tobias was still outside.

He was. Unfortunately, she wasn't. I guess I should've said something about her trifling ass Mama and her perverted ass Daddy. That surely would've gotten her ass over here.

Until next time...

"Hey. What's going on? I've tried to call you back. You haven't picked up," Ray said as soon as I opened the front door.

I just stood there, looking at him.

"Is this about that charm and April?"

"You tell me."

"There's nothing to tell. I've never touched her. I love you. I've always loved you Tiffany," he said.

I shrugged my shoulders.

"I just need a little space," I said and tried to close the door, but he stopped it.

"Space from what? Me? What have I done to you? Other than try to be here for you?"

"I'll call you when I need you, okay?" I tried to shut the door again, but he wouldn't allow me to.

"You'll call me when you need me?"

"Yeah. Just let me be, Ray. I'm stressed and I have a lot on mind. The look on his face scared me.

"You know what? I've tried to do things your way," Ray said.

I looked at him as though he'd lost his mind.

"I tried telling you how I feel about you. I tried being there for you. I tried always being available and coming to your rescue. I tried licking your pussy to relieve some stress. But nothing is ever enough."

He pushed the door, hard, and started to walk closer and closer to me as I backed away.

"I appreciate what you've done."

"No. You don't. Instead, you ignore me. Tell me you need some space. Act like I'm bothering you. And you try to accuse me of doing something with your sister. I've never laid a finger on her. On either of them. Well…"

I didn't like the way that he'd said well.

I knew that something was coming after it and I knew that I wasn't going to like it.

"Do you know that Shelly hates you?"

I looked at him confused.

"She's jealous of you. She has been since we were married. Your own sister can't stand the ground that you walk on. You're the pretty one. The successful one. I can see why she would be envious of you."

"What are you talking about? Shelly isn't jealous of me."

"Once I started trying to prove to you that Tobias wasn't who he said that he was, I started following him. Not often, but when I had the spare time. I saw him meet up with Brian, your sister's husband. At first, I thought that maybe they were getting together to hang out because they were married to sisters, but then one day, I saw a money transaction. Tobias gave him a bag and then I saw Brian pull out a stack of money. I thought it was drug related. I jumped at the idea of sending Tobias to prison. Away from you."

Ray was standing right in front of me. The dog stepped in between us, and Ray stepped back.

"As you know, I was digging around on Tobias. Once I seen the little exchange, I found that your sister and Brian have a house phone. So I tapped it. I wanted to see if he and Tobias ever talked. But they never used it much. But one day, your sister did. She asked Brian why he wasn't answering his cellphone and then she told him what she'd told you. Something about a mask and that she'd told you that he'd wanted her to convince you to marry Tobias. She then asked him about the money that Tobias had given him. She asked if they were going to get more for sending you around in circles, trying to throw you off and keep you confused."

I shook my head.

No. No. He's lying.

"She disgusts me. I've never liked her all that much anyway. You see, I love you. I love you enough to protect

92

you. Defend you. I'll do anything for you. But she. She's your own flesh and blood and it bothered me to see her doing you like that. I didn't know exactly what they were all a part of, but her involvement, made me sick. So, I took care of it."

I looked at him confused. He waited to see if I would ask him the question to the answer that I already knew the answer to.

"You shot Shelly?"

He nodded.

"That bitch deserves to die. She's ungrateful. She doesn't know the value of family. Or love. You protect the people that you love. That's what I was doing Strawberry. Protecting you. From her. From an enemy that you didn't even know that you had. I did the deed. Cleaned up the scene and said it was a drive by."

He sounded so sincere about something so wrong.

He could have killed her! I just couldn't believe my ears.

"Don't I at least get a thank you?"

"For what? For almost killing my sister?" I growled.

"I was trying to do you a favor. She doesn't love you. She doesn't care about you. But I do. I care about you. I love you."

"If you loved me, you would've shot Tobias. Not my freaking sister!"

I thought that I would just throw that out there. Just in case he wanted to help a sista' out or something.

"I would if that's what you wanted me to do. It would be my pleasure. I love you that much Strawberry."

I was frozen in place. I was still trying to wrap my mind around his confession. Was he telling the truth about Shelly? Replaying Brian's comments at the hospital, I was sure that he was. But he had no right to shoot her. He should have come to me. I would've handle her. In my own way. He could've killed her! And he'd just stated that he would help me get rid of Tobias. And now I wasn't sure of what reaction I wanted to display. Be pissed for what he did to Shelly? Or hide my anger and discuss what he was willing to do to Tobias?

"Say something. I was just trying to help. I love you. Do you love me?"

Honestly, I wished that Ray hadn't told me what he'd done. He was yet another person in my life that I felt like I didn't really know.

"Say that you love me Strawberry. Tell me that you love me too," Ray pleaded. "I was protecting you. I love you. I was looking out for you. Tell me that you love me too," he said again and I could see that he was getting frustrated.

"Say it!" Ray screamed and fear took over my body, and I tried to run towards my purse, but Ray grabbed me by my hair.

"Where are you going huh?" he said pulling me towards him.

The dog barked and lunged towards him, but Ray kicked him. Hard. Sending him flying across the living room. I watched Killer try to stand to his feet, but he whimpered and laid on his side.

"I love you. I've given up everything for you. I could lose my job for what I did for you. I couldn't make my new marriage work because of you. I never moved away because of you. I've always loved you. Now tell me that you love me too," Ray said in my ear.

Oh God. Tobias was right. He is obsessed!

"Ray, let go of my hair! You're hurting me," I pleaded.

"Say it. Say that you love me Strawberry."

"I love you okay. I really do. Thank you for what you did for me. Now please let me go."

I waited for Ray to release my hair but he didn't.

"You walk around here, with this big ole' belly, carrying a baby by some other man. He doesn't love you like I do. Nobody loves you like I do Tiffany!"

You're right. Nobody loves me like you do psychopath!

"I always make sure you're safe. I watch over your house. Check around. Ride by. Sometimes I stand by your bedroom window. Just so that I can be close to you while you sleep. I do all of this because I love you. Don't you see that?"

I wondered how many times I'd thought that it was someone else snooping around, when in actuality it was him.

"Ray. Okay. I understand. Now please let me go."

He didn't seem to be listening to me. It was as though he had gone into some crazy rant, and the only thing he was able to hear was himself.

"I love you woman!"

"Ray. Let go of my hair!"

Still, he ignored me. And then…

"She asked you nicely. I on the other hand, I'm not so nice," he said.

Tobias.

Ray froze and looked at him and so did I. I never thought that I would be so happy to see him, of all people, but at that moment, I was. But Ray still didn't let go of my hair.

"We can do this the easy way. Or the hard way," Tobias said. He lifted his shirt so that Ray could get a glimpse of his gun. I didn't even know that he had one. But of course he did. He was an undercover criminal.

"I doubt that you are going to shoot a cop."

"Maybe not; if you were just a cop. But you're not. You're an obsessive, trespassing, abusive ex-husband, harassing his pregnant ex-wife, and just so happens; you're a cop too."

Ray let go of my hair and I scrambled towards my purse.

"I'm the wrong one for you to fuck with," Ray growled.

"No. I am. Now, not only do I have footage of you creeping around her house late at night; that video credit goes to my wife. But I also took the liberty of recording about a minute of your last little episode. Insane cop, harassing pregnant ex-wife would make a hell of a headline and embarrass the hell out of the department. Don't you think? Not only have you lost the girl, but you'll lose your job too. And fucking you up, right here, right now, would be just to make me feel better," Tobias stood like he was some kind of gangster or thug or something.

It almost turned me on.

Ray chuckled and turned to look at me but I was now holding my gun. Pointing it at his head.

"Get the hell out of here! And if you ever, ever come near me again, I'll kill you!" I pulled the trigger and released a bullet only inches away from his head. He looked at me, knowing that I could have made the shot.

Ray looked defeated and then he turned away and made his way towards the door. He glanced back at me one last time, and then he was gone.

And so was Tobias.

****

Chapter SIX

"Strawberry, I'm worried about you. Shelly has been asking for you. Why haven't you been to the hospital?"

I just held the phone.

After the little incident with Ray, I didn't know who I could trust. I felt like the entire world was against me, or at least out to get me. Except for Mama.

"You heard some of the things that Brian said Mama. And I've just been going through a lot. With the baby coming soon, and the divorce. I just need some time to myself for a while. That's all. I'll be fine."

Mama said a few encouraging words and then she said goodbye. Minutes later, Shelly's number appeared, but I pressed ignore. I was sure that Ray had been telling the truth about her. But he still had no right to shoot her. Hell, he should have let me do it. I was so mad at her. Or maybe I was disappointed in her. Whatever it was, I didn't need to talk to her or be around her. I couldn't trust myself around all of that hospital equipment. Fooling with me, her breathing machine might "accidentally" get unplugged.

I headed to look out the window. As always, Tobias was parked in the driveway. I no longer fussed about him being there and I'd had no choice but to thank him for stepping in when he did the other night.

Had he not been there, I wasn't sure what Ray would've done to me. And now I felt somewhat obligated to be just a little nicer to him. Not too nice to make him think that everything was okay between us. But I mean potentially, maybe he had saved my life.

I decided to make some hot chocolate. After pouring two cups, I managed to fit into one of my jackets and then I headed outside.

It was about 9 o'clock at night. Tobias looked at me, strangely, and then he rolled down his car window.

"Here."

He took the hot chocolate out of my hand. He allowed his hand to brush up against mine.

No. No. Get thee behind me Satan! I will not start to feel anything for him again. Nope! Nope! Nope!

"How are you feeling?"

Usually I would be a smart ass, but I shrugged.

"Fine. Just thought to bring you a cup."

"Thanks."

I turned to walk away, but he called my name.

"Can we chat for a second?"

I heard him unlock his car doors. It had been a while now, and every night, he was there. Sleeping in the car. Watching over my house. Even if I didn't hear from him or even if I didn't see him all day long, every night before bed, I would look outside, and he would be there.

I wondered what his wife had to say about all of this. I was sure that she wasn't too happy about it. But she hadn't called my phone or been by the house. But I knew that it was only a matter of time.

I made my way around to the passenger side of his car and got in.

"I've been thinking."

I didn't know if that was a good thing.

"I know how you feel about me. I ain't saying that you shouldn't. I ain't saying that you should forget that I played you. But, just let me be a father to my son. I'll never let anything happen to him. I never had a daddy and I just want to be there."

I just looked at him.

"Everything that I have ever really cared about is on the line. If I stay here, I'll probably lose my wife. The one woman, the only woman, that I have ever truly loved. But the man in me won't let me turn my back on him. A part of me died with my son. Since then, something has always been missing. I'm not trying to replace him with this baby, but I won't fail him. I won't fail like I did the first time. I'll never take my eye off of him."

I wondered if Tobias was going to become emotional. I really couldn't handle that right now. But he didn't.

"I'm not a good guy. I know that. You know that. But he is the best part of me."

Why couldn't he have been a normal husband?

Why did he have to come with all of the lies, games, and a veteran wife; making this situation harder than it had to be?

And now he wanted me to bend. He wanted me to forgive. It was as though he couldn't see that he'd hurt me. It was as though he didn't realize that I was the one with the short end of the stick.

"Tobias what you did to me, how you played me. I just don't know."

I tried to focus on hating him. But honestly, the more and more time that passed, I didn't. I just didn't have the energy. I hadn't thought about killing him, since he'd stepped in with the Ray situation. I was just over it all. I just wanted to take my money and run away. And you know what, that was just what I was going to do.

All of this happened as a result of something that I'd done. I had to accept that. Live with that. And now it was time to move on.

The baby kicked. Placing my hot chocolate in the cup holder, I grabbed his hand and led it to my belly. I placed my hand on top of his as the baby tossed and turned and kicked me over and over again. Tobias giggled.

"Hey son."

Ugh. I felt like I was going to be all mushy and stuff. Emotional walls, Tiffany. He definitely doesn't deserve your sympathy. I didn't care if he was trying to be a better man. I didn't care if he'd saved me. And I didn't care if he was sleeping outside in the car every night to make sure that he could protect me. He was still a snake. He still couldn't be trusted.

Neither of us said anything for a while and then I reached for the door handle, but he grabbed my hand. He stared at me. I stared back. I hadn't looked at him with anything other than pure disgust in a very long time, but for the first time, I actually saw him as more than just a walking, talking, pile of shit. I actually saw his face. He looked stressed. Not that I should care. But it was noticeable.

He placed his hand underneath my chin.

Oh hell no. What do he think he's doing?

He looked deep into my eyes.

"Even if you never forgive me. From the bottom of my heart, I'm sorry."

I didn't say anything and he didn't let go of my chin.

"Strawberry---" But before he could finish his sentence, a car horn wailed behind us. I screeched in fear, and Tobias glanced behind him. The car lights were bright, almost blinding. The horn continued to scream as Tobias opened his door and so did I. I didn't even have to look back at the car, I knew exactly who it was. His wife.

"Strawberry, just go in the house. Please," he said and he headed to the car. And even though I didn't want to, even though I had a bone to pick with her, I listened to him and I headed towards the house in the opposite direction.

~***~

Tobias Speaks...Again...

"I suggest you keep your ass at this house tonight," she scowled me. I just looked at her. Ray hadn't ridden by Strawberry's in a long while, so she was probably safe.

Besides, I'd seen her shoot. She could protect herself.

"Cool," I said to Fran and she rolled her eyes and headed to shower. Man. Things between us ain't ever been so damn bad. All we do is fuss, fight, and fuck. Fuss until she threw the first punch. And then we would make-up. I had to give it to her though, she loved the hell out of me.

She still didn't like the situation, but she was trying. She threatened to leave me every day, but she was still here. But she wasn't taking what I was dishing out quietly. Every damn day, I had to hear her mouth.

And we still had about two months to go. And I still didn't have a real plan. My main focus was to make sure that the baby got here. I would figure everything else out later.

I sat there for a while, and then she came out. She was naked, and I admired her frame.

"I love you," I said to my wife but she didn't say it back. Instead she said. "Could've fooled me. I'm starting to think you love her more." I watched her lotion her body and climb into bed. I turned my head and looked out the window.

I'm starting to think that I do too.

~***~

"Have you heard from April?" Mama asked concerned.

"No. I haven't. Why?"

"I went by her apartment today. She moved. I went by the school and they told me she withdrew."

What?

"They said that they've been trying to contact you to pick up a check. Something about they didn't need the full tuition since she left."

"Ma, let me call you back."

I called April. No answer.

Tapping my fingers, I thought about the last time I saw her. She's gotten mad before and shut herself away, but she quit school? Now, something definitely wasn't right.

I called her again. Still no answer and then I thought about my money. I looked in my purse for my spare card to April's account. I'd moved half of my money to her account when I thought that Tobias was going to try to find a way to take it. I punched the numbers in and waited for the automated woman to tell me my fate.

"Your balance in this account is zero dollars and zero cents."

What?

I went to online banking. Since it was technically April's account, of course I wasn't notified of any type of withdrawals or activity. April knew that I was hiding it from Tobias because I'd told her but never had she touched it without asking first.

Pulling up her account information, I confirmed the zero balance. I checked the dates and saw that she'd emptied the account over a week ago.

Where is she? And where the hell is my money?

****

Chapter SEVEN

"Hey, um, is Tiffany here?"

Some old man, carrying flowers had just knocked on my door.

"I'm Tiffany."

It was lunch-time."

"Oh. Um, I didn't know that you were pregnant."

"Excuse me?"

"I'm Lou. From the dating site. The one that you talked to yesterday. The one that you sent the nudes too and uh, the phone sex. You told me to meet you here today, so we could go to lunch. You told me to bring you daisies."

What?

"I'm sorry. You must have the wrong person."

"No. I don't. See."

He pulled out his phone.

"You texted me the address. And your tits. And your..."

"I get it. But that's not me. That's not my number."

"Oh, I get it. You like to play games with people."

"What? No."

Before he could say something else, another car pulled into the driveway. A short black man got out, carrying daisies. Another car pulled in behind him and I waited to see who got out of it. This man was white, and he too was carrying daisies.

Without saying anything else, I shut my door and locked it. Lou pressed on the doorbell, but I called Tobias.

"Could you come? Now!"

Sadly, he was the only person that I could call for help.

I looked out the window and there were now twelve random men standing in my front yard. All of them were holding daises. They seemed to be chatting, as Lou continued to ring the doorbell. My phone started to ring and though the number wasn't saved, I recognized it.

I picked it up and listened.

She was laughing. Hard. I knew that it was Tobias's wife. She didn't say anything. All she did was laugh. Of course she'd had something to do with this. I hung up the phone and tried to calm myself down. She was an even bigger pain in the ass than Tobias had been when he had been trying to get me to leave him.

By the time Tobias got there, it was over forty men outside of my house. All of them claimed to have spoken to me the day before. All of them had the same nude pictures. All of them claimed to have had phone sex. And all of them were carrying flowers.

It took a while, but finally Tobias got all of them to leave and then he headed back to his car.

"Wait. You're coming back tonight right?" I asked him. Hell, what if one of them came back?

"Yes," was all that he said, before getting into his car and driving away.

~***~

"Braxton-Hicks."

"Already?"

"Well, you're right at eight months. So, it's normal. Just go home. Get plenty of rest. And try not to stress. Maybe relieve some stress, if you know what I mean," the doctor chuckled. Tobias and I looked at each other uncomfortably. After a few more minutes, it was time to go.

Tobias helped me to the car and he took me home.

"Sit down, ill fix you something to drink." .

I had been definitely stressed lately. My little sister was pretty much missing. And so was some of my money. Mama was worried out of her mind. I was still avoiding Shelly. Ray had called me, creeping me out, saying that no matter what, I'll always be his baby. He acted as though he hadn't done anything wrong. And not to mention that Tobias's wife was working my last nerve! Some of the stuff that she had been doing, I would've never thought of. I just didn't know how much more nonsense I could take.

And the crazy part of it all was that I felt myself depending on Tobias again. I didn't really have anyone else. I didn't have anybody but him.

"Have you picked a name for him yet?"

I observed Tobias. I'd thought about naming him after my dad. But I wasn't sure.

"No."

Tobias didn't say anything. He reached me a glass of cold water and started to rub my feet.

"You don't have to do that."

"You're the mother of my child. I'll do anything for you," he said.

I never knew how to respond to him these days. He was always trying to be nice or helpful but I won't forget, I can't forget what he done to me. And his wife made sure that I would always remember.

Briefly, he rubbed my feet.

"Have you ever…"

"What?"

"Have you ever thought about us? Like a family?"

"What?" I questioned Tobias.

"I mean, I know it's crazy. But what if we could be a family?"

"Are you crazy? Have you forgotten the bull crap you took me through?"

"No. I didn't forget. But we can start over."

"Start over? Who? You? Me? The baby? And you wife?"

"That's the only problem."

I looked at him strangely.

"Oh so now she's a problem? I didn't know that she was a problem."

"She's not. It's just. I don't know."

"You love her right?"

"More than anything in the world."

"But?"

Tobias was quiet.

Just as he was about to say something, there was a knock at the door. I shook my head and wobbled in that direction. Looking out the peep hole, I was confused. I opened the door.

"What are you doing here? How do you know where I live?" I asked to her. She just looked at me.

I waited for a few seconds, and finally, she spoke.

"Where is my husband?" she said nastily.

What? My mouth opened wide.

"Your husband?"

Tobias stood up.

"Yes. My stupid ass husband," she said.

I backed away from the door. I was still in shock. I couldn't believe that she was his wife.

Tobias's wife is…the janitor.

The janitor from my old job. Now it all made sense!

Tobias said she found me. She was always watching me work late. She had to have known that I was alone. She had to have known that I didn't have a husband or kids. And not to mention all of the late night, office conversations with Shelly. She had to have overheard. She was why Tobias saw me with the flat tire. She probably flattened it on her way in. She was the one that let Tobias in that night to have sex with me. And I'm sure she was the one to record our little rendezvous. Everything just made sense. And she was at the wedding. Remember? She was at our damn wedding! I told her that I was pregnant. She had to be the one to destroy the bathroom. Oh goodness! I just can't believe that it's her! And looking down at her feet, she was wearing the pink tennis shoes…from the gym. The shoes that I saw just before the burning paper towels came flying underneath the stall.

It was her. The janitor. Tobias wife.

"You?"

"Me."

Tobias stood between us.

"Fran, what are you doing here baby?"

"What are you doing here?"

"She needed to go to the hospital."

"Is the baby dead?"

I gasped and touched my stomach. I wondered if I could reach across Tobias and punch her in the mouth.

"No," Tobias said.

"Damn," she pouted.

She stared at me and my stomach.

"No one is here. Let me whoop her ass, kick her in the stomach a few times and we can disappear."

"No Fran. No."

"Why?"

"You already know why. Because of the baby."

"It's not our baby! I don't care about that bastard baby!"

She yelled and I felt like things might get out of hand. Killer just stood there. I waited for him to start barking, or trying to attack her, but he didn't. I guess he'd learned his lesson last time to stay the hell out of the way.

"Go home Fran. We will talk when I get there."

"No. We will talk now. I can give you a baby. We don't need hers. She's not going to give you her baby. Don't you know that by now? Let's just go."

Give him my baby? You damn right I'm not giving him my baby!

"Fran. Go home."

"Only if you come with me."

"Okay. I'll come with you."

"For good. No more coming over here seeing about her and this baby, let's go home, pack up and hit the road. Let's go start a new life like we planned to before all of this. We still have some money. We can start something and make more money. Let's just go." She reached out her hand, but Tobias didn't take it.

"I'm not leaving my son behind Fran."

I could tell that her heart was breaking just by the look on her face. They stared at each other for a while and then she spoke.

"It's me…or them. Right here. Right now. You have to choose."

"I choose you…and the baby."

She stared at him and then looked at me.

"Wrong answer," she said, and with that she turned and walked away.

Tobias stood there. Staring at the door. After a while, he took a deep breath and then opened the door.

"I'll be in the car if you need me."

~***~

"Police! Open up!"

I opened the door and a squad of police officers came running through my front door.

"What's going on?"

They ran in every direction of my house and no one answered my question. Killer was barking like crazy.

Finally, a man in a suit came in.

"Who are you?"

"The owner of this house. What the hell is going on?"

"We got a call that you are running a human trafficking ring out of here. We were told that you had about ten little girl victims, all under the age of fourteen. Ma'am are there any little girls in here?"

"What?"

"Answer the question ma'am."

"No. No there aren't any little girls in here. And I'm not involved in human trafficking. Where the hell did you get that from?"

"I can't tell you that ma'am. Just stay put while we search the house."

It was early in the morning and looking outside, Tobias's car was gone. I heard things breaking and falling over the next ten minutes or so. Finally, the man came back over to me.

"I'm sorry. There must have been some kind of mistake."

"Oh, you can bet your sweet ass that there was. Don't be surprise if your station hears from my lawyer."

"Ma'am that won't be necessary. We were just doing our job. You have a good day now," he said as the men cleared out of my house. They all gathered and talked outside of my house for a while. I watched them in disbelief. Finally, the cars loaded up and they all started to head out. And that's when I saw her. Tobias's wife Fran was standing on the sidewalk, across the street from my house, with her arms folded over her chest.

I should've known that it was her who had sent them. She wasn't going to be satisfied until I whooped her ass! We made eye contact, briefly, but it didn't last long. She started to walk down the street and without looking back, she disappeared.

If she wasn't the definition of crazy in love, I didn't know what was. But she was asking for trouble and believe me; she'd found it.

I dialed Tobias's number with a smile on my face.

"Hey, I'm not feeling well. Can you come over?"

She could huff. She could puff. But one thing she couldn't deny was that as of right now and as long as this baby was in my belly, Tobias was in my corner. I had the power. And I was about to show her just what to do with it.

~***~

"She's gorgeous."

"Thank you. What are you having? You look like you are about to pop."

"A boy. And I'm so ready to get this over with."

"Yea. I remember the feeling," she smiled at me, but I could tell that her smile was fake. It was like she was trying to read me or something.

I looked past her at the sight of Fran standing beside the vegetables. She was following me everywhere these days and she wasn't trying to hide it. I went to the salon yesterday, she came in and sat to watch me until someone told her that she either had to get something done to her hair or go. I drove up to see Mama. When I came out, she was parked on the side of the road. I had about five pictures in my phone of her following me. As far as I was concerned, she was now considered a stalker, and my life could be in danger. So, whatever happens to her, I hope the courts are able to see that I was only defending myself.

"That woman has been following me," I said to the woman that I had been talking to. Putting it on the record. She didn't respond. She turned to see who I was talking about. Both of us stood looking at Tobias's wife, Fran, as she walked by the potatoes and then she stopped by the onions. She picked one up.

"Bitch I wish you would," I mumbled.

Fran smirked and I knew that she was going to throw it. And she did.

I dodged one, but the second one that she threw, hit me on the side of the face.

"I am going to whoop your ass!" I started walking towards her, but she fired another. And then another one. She was aiming them at my stomach and I kept turning so that the onions would hit me in the back instead.

Every time I turned to walk towards her, she threw another one at my stomach. And then she started putting on a show for the crowd.

"This woman is pregnant by my husband!" she screamed.

I froze as everyone started to whisper.

"Yep. Pregnant by a married man. Wives, guard your husbands. She just might come after yours next!" She bellowed and grabbed a hand full of grapes as she walked towards the exit.

Embarrassed, I just stood there. I started to cry. Not because I was sad, but because I was so damn mad!

Ohhh…she was going to get it! I was going to kill her. I was going to kill her!

"Are you okay?"

I didn't answer the woman who was now touching my hand.

"Is it true what she said?"

I still didn't say anything, but I felt her put a card in my hand.

"My name is Hannah. I used to be a psychologist, now I do a little counseling, when I can. If you ever need someone to talk to, give me a call," she said and her and her precious little girl walked away.

I dropped her card on my way out the door. I didn't need to talk to anyone. It was time for some action.

I hurried home and instead of cooking like I'd planned, since I didn't get my groceries, I ordered out and then I waited on Tobias to pull up outside. Right on time.

If this is how she wanted to do things, then it was time for me to get on her level. It was time for me to take the one thing, the only thing, that she cared about.

Tobias.

"Could you come here for a second?"

I watched him get out of the car and head to the door.

"What's wrong?"

"I'm not feeling good. I have terrible back pain. And my feet are swollen and aching like crazy." I didn't even tell him what happened at the grocery store with his wife. If she told him, cool. If she didn't, that's fine too. As long as her darling husband put his hands all over my body, that's all that mattered.

"Okay. I'll make you some tea and rub your feet. Do you have a heating pad? Are you allowed to use them?"

"No. I don't think so. But a massage might work."

He nodded and headed to fix me some tea.

"Maybe I should take a hot bath first."

I headed to the bathroom to run my bath water. I washed quickly and then came out, dripping wet, without a towel. Tobias was now in my bedroom.

"Uh, your tea is on the dresser."

"Thank you."

I headed towards it. I took a sip. I smiled because I knew that Tobias was probably looking at my ass.

Yes! Look at all that ass boy! Pregnancy had definitely given me a big ole' round, juicy booty. And I bent over so that he could get a good view of it.

"You want to do my back or my feet first?"

"It's up to you."

I walked towards him as he sat on the edge of my bed.

"I can't lay on my stomach for the massage. It's too big. I'm just going to get on all fours, you know like in doggy-style position, so you can reach it." Tobias glared at me like I was crazy.

"It hurt so bad. Sorry to be naked. I just need you to try to take the pain away. I can't focus."

"Okay. Let me try to help you."

Tobias put his phone on the table beside my bed as I bent over on my knees. I giggled to myself. He was going to be as hard as a rock. He touched my back.

"Ouch," I said. It was a little sore from that crazy woman hitting me with the onions.

"Damn. Where did these bruises come from?"

"I don't know. Just make it feel better," I said, low and sexy. After a few minutes, his phone started to vibrate on the table. I knew that it was her.

"My knees hurt a little. Let me lay on my side."

Tobias moved and I laid on my side up near his phone.

"Get a little bit of that lotion and massage it with that."

Tobias headed to the dresser and I pressed the green button since his phone was vibrating again.

Tobias came back and got to work.

"Ohh! That feels so good. I really needed this." I was loud. I knew that she was listening. "Ohhhhhhhh," I cooed.

Tobias didn't have a clue as to what I was doing. I could tell that he was really trying to make me feel better. I whined as though I was in so much pain and for the next fifteen minutes or so, I had his full attention.

Finally, I laid on my back and he sat down and grabbed my feet.

"Thank you."

"You don't have to thank me. You don't have anyone else to do it Strawberry," he said as he focused on rubbing my feet. Slowly, I opened my legs more and more. I caught him glancing at my pussy cat, once or twice.

His phone was vibrating again so she must've hung up and was trying to get him to answer. He had to hear it because I did. But he didn't answer it.

"Okay. What else do you need?"

"Nothing. Just you."

"What?"

"I mean can you lay with me until I fall asleep? I've been having bad dreams for the past few nights. Just until I fall asleep."

Tobias shrugged.

"Ain't you gonna' put some clothes on?"

"No. I'm hot. If I'm too hot, the baby seems to move all night long."

Tobias nodded and took off his shoes. He got in the bed beside me. He didn't touch me and he wasn't too close. I glanced at one of my windows. I'd kept the blinds open on one single window on purpose. I already knew that she was going to come by. I was hoping that she started snooping around. I wanted her to see. I know what this would look like and I wanted her to see him in bed with me.

We didn't speak. We just laid in silence. He actually ended up falling asleep first and I rolled over and looked at his phone.

13 Missed Calls,

I snickered, laid the phone back down and closed my eyes.

"Come outside," Tobias said the next morning.

Not only was his car all messed up but she had spray painted "Whore" on my garage door.

All of my neighbors were standing around talking and pointing at it. And then there was a doll. A naked, black doll. Hanging by a sheet, on the tree that was in the middle of the yard. A knife was in its chest.

I just stood there. At this point, nothing she did surprised me. But no matter what she did, I wanted her to know that I wasn't scared of her. And looking at Tobias's face expression, and the vein popping out of the side of his neck, I knew that I didn't have to be.

Ooooh. She was going to get in trouble!

~***~

"Can I take a shower?" Tobias asked.

I looked at him as though he'd just asked me for a million bucks.

"She won't let me come home."

I shrugged and he headed to the bathroom.

Tobias disappeared to the back of the house and I continued to clean. After washing the dishes, I opened the blinds on the patio door.

"Ahh!" I screamed and grabbed my chest.

Tobias's wife was just standing there.

She didn't move. She didn't try to hide.

She just stood there.

I looked at her and after a second or two, she smiled.

"What? What is it? What's wrong?" Tobias was soak and wet and running in my direction. I turned my attention back to her and watched her as she scanned Tobias from top to bottom. I could see the anger in her eyes. I could damn near feel her pain.

Tobias held up his hands, and the towel fell.

"No. No. It's not what it looks like. I promise. It's not what it looks like," he shouted but I was sure that she couldn't hear him.

"Fuck!" Tobias screamed and ran back towards the bathroom.

She and I stared each other down for a while. I wanted to get under her skin so I winked at her and then I licked my lips. Surprisingly, the crazy bitch did it back and then she took out a knife. She started to drag it across the patio doors, smiling, and then she disappeared.

Damn nut case!

Moments later, he came running back up the hall and out the front door. He didn't say goodbye. He didn't say anything. He was gone. And looking outside, she was too.

For the rest of the day, Tobias didn't call to check on me and he didn't come back that night to sleep in the driveway.

Oh well.

****

Chapter EIGHT

"You've been avoiding me," Shelly said, walking into Mama's house. I felt like it was a set up. Mama walked out of the room and I heard her bedroom door close.

"I don't have anything to say to you."

"You know, when I woke up, like really woke up, the first person I looked for was you."

"I'm surprised."

"What do you know?" She asked as though she wasn't planning to deny anything.

"I know that you lied to me and that you were playing me the whole time. You knew what Brian had done for Tobias. You knew what Tobias was doing to me. And you let it happen. You said nothing. As far as I'm concerned, you my love, were better off dead."

I knew that comment was harsh, but I didn't care. She deserved it.

"Yes. I knew. I was torn. He's my husband. You're my sister."

"That's right. Your own flesh and blood. I would have given you anything you asked me for. You knew that. So why?"

"Brian. He told me we needed the money. He threatened to leave me if I couldn't be his backbone when he needed me to. He said you wouldn't get hurt, at least not physically, and that he needed my help. You know how hard it was for me to find love. And unlike you, I was always looking. After all of the failed relationships, Brian came along. I guess I just didn't want to lose him. I didn't know about it all at first. By the time that he filled me in completely, you and Tobias were already married. I didn't know about Tobias's other wife until the day of the wedding."

No matter what she said, nothing would ever change the fact that I would never trust her again. I would never look at her the same.

"You're my sister. I do love you even though what I did was a hell of a way of showing it. Forgive me?"

"Probably not. I'm pregnant by someone else's husband. I don't know what will happen, but there is a good chance that my son may grow up without a father because of something that you and your husband were a part of. So, excuse me if I don't feel any sympathy for a grown ass woman who only cares about herself and her piece of shit of a mate," I stood to leave, but Shelly stood too.

"I'm sorry Strawberry. If I could take it back, I would."

"You can't. And the only thing that I'm sorry about is that Ray didn't kill you."

"Ray?"

"Yes. He shot you. He told me himself. You said that you saw who shot you. It was Ray right?"

Shelly shook her head.

"No. Ray didn't shoot me Strawberry. It was April."

What?

~***~

"Why are you crying?"

"My life is such a mess."

April shot Shelly. Well, accidentally. Shelly said that somehow, April found out that Shelly knew about what Brian and Tobias was doing to me. She said that she had no idea how she found out but that she was waiting on her after work that evening. April told her that she'd heard that Tobias was using me, playing me and cheating on me, and that she knew that Shelly knew about it. Shelly said that she tried to deny it but that April got in her face and told her that she was going to tell me. The gun was Shelly's. She said she pulled out the gun and told April that she had better keep her mouth shut. She said of course she wasn't going to shoot her, she was just wanted to scare her. Though April never said much, Shelly said she just had a feeling that even pulling out the gun on her wasn't going to work. So, she said she called me in front of April, to try to cover her ass. To beat her to the punch. She said that April tried to take the phone out of her hand and they started to scuffle, forgetting that Shelly was holding the gun. And then the gun went off.

Tobias just looked at me, but I was still in my thoughts.

Shelly said that April started to panic and started to apologize. Before she blacked out, she told April to call Ray, tell him what happened and get him to fix it. From there we can only assume that April told Ray what happened. And since April was still missing, I hadn't had a choice but to call Ray and ask him myself. After he apologized to me over and over again for his behavior, finally I got him to talk. He admitted that he was covering for April. He admitted that he cleaned up the crime scene and made it look like a drive-by. He also admitted that he shot Shelly two more times. He said that it was to make it look like a drive-by but I think that he did it hoping that she was dead. April left her charm at the scene. He picked it up. That's why he had the charm. Not because they were having sex.

I had a headache. All I could think about was April. She probably already felt so much guilt for making the gun go off and I just made it worse by saying that she was screwing Ray. My family was torn apart. I hated one sister. I needed to apologize to the other. But it had been forever since anyone had heard from April and I had a feeling that she was gone. Forever. I had a feeling that she'd taken my money and that she was just gone. She'd always been different. I could see why she would just run away and never look back. Lord knows, that exactly what I wanted to do.

"Don't stress remember."

"Easy for you to say."

"No. It's not." Tobias.

I was going to ask, but I didn't care what was going on with him and his woman. I had enough things to worry about.

"Let Killer out to go to the bathroom for me please."

Tobias nodded, opened the door and Killer ran out.

"Um, about the other night."

"What about it?"

"You answered my phone, while Fran was calling didn't you?"

"I don't know what you're talking about," I said. Surprisingly, Tobias smiled. He opened the door and called for Killer. He got quiet and went outside. I followed him.

He stood on the porch and once I made it to his side, I saw my dog, Killer, lying on the ground., with the knife in his side.

Poor dog!

Tobias's wife glared at the both of us, from her car on the side of the street. She rolled up her window but she didn't pull off. I didn't say anything. I didn't move.

Tobias answered his phone and she screamed in his ear once he answered it.

"Well, don't just stand there! Bring your ass here!" she screamed. Tobias walked off the porch, stepped over the dog, and headed in her direction.

She's out of control and she needs to be stopped. And I was going to stop her.

~***~

"Tobias!"

I opened the front door. I flicked the light switch on and off. "Tobias!"

I couldn't breathe. Everything was starting to spin, and I couldn't keep my eyes open. I forced myself to sit down to keep from falling on the floor. I didn't want the baby to get hurt. I tried to scream again but nothing came out. I was passing out…

"How you feeling?"

"Woozy."

"As you should. I want to go over your testing with you."

I touched my stomach. The baby was still cutting cartwheels in my stomach. Good. He was fine.

"We found Penicillin in your system. Aren't you allergic to Penicillin?"

I looked at the nurse.

"Yes. Yes I am."

"Why did you take it? Are you trying to kill yourself?" The nurse asked.

"What? No. I wasn't. I didn't take any Penicillin."

"Well, the test results found Penicillin in your system. And the reports were also positive for Xanax."

Xanax?

Where in the hell would I get Xanax?

"Oh no. You must have the charts mixed up. I'm pregnant. I wouldn't have taken a Xanax."

"But you would have taken it if you weren't?"

"What? No? I'm not saying that. I didn't take a Xanax or Penicillin!"

"But it's in your bloodwork and test results."

Tobias was standing right beside of me. Immediately I turned on him.

"What did you do? What did you do?"

"Nothing Strawberry. I swear. You know that I would never hurt my son." He was calm and he was waiting on the nurse to say her next words.

"We reported this to Child Welfare Services."

"What? You reported what? I did not take Xanax! I'm pregnant!"

I felt dizzy so I laid my head back on the hospital bed.

"Xanax is a serious drug and cause harm to the baby. I'm not sure what their actions will be but I will have to recommend that they do what's in the best interest of the child. Try to get some rest. They should be here to talk to you more about it shortly."

Silently I cried.

"What did you do Tobias?" I sobbed.

"I swear. I didn't do anything. You know that I wouldn't hurt the baby. Let's think. Did you take anything? I know you've been having headaches and the doctor said that you could talk certain medicines. Did you take something else?"

Tobias was eager to hear my response. I could tell in his voice.

"No. No. No. No! The only thing I took was my prenatal vitamins. I'd forgotten to take them earlier. I noticed them on the sink and popped two of them. That was it. A few minutes later, I started feeling funny and I made my way to the front door to signal you for help. I wouldn't take anything to hurt the baby. I swear."

"Well the pills didn't just jump into your system Strawberry," Tobias sounded as if he was blaming me.

"I didn't take them. I didn't take anything to hurt the baby!" I shouted as Child Welfare entered the room.

I wouldn't hurt my baby.

~***~

"Stop calling me Ray."

"I miss you. I'm sorry."

"Please. Just stop calling me okay."

I hung up the phone.

"Are you ready for this?"

"I'm as ready as I'll every be," I said to Tobias who had just walked into the room.

We were packing my bags for the hospital. I was going to be induced the next day. I was nervous. I was nervous about delivery. Nervous about holding him in my arms for the first time. And I was definitely nervous about Child Welfare being in the mix. The incident happened over a week ago, and I didn't know what they planned to do, but they weren't going to take my baby. I would spend every dime that I had to fight for him. I didn't do drugs. I still didn't know how the drugs got in my system. I hadn't been around anyone. No one could've slipped it in my food or drink. I checked my prenatal vitamins, they hadn't given me the wrong prescription. So really, I just didn't know. But I was sure that either Tobias or his wife had something to do with it. Since the medicine could've harmed the baby, I would have to say that it was probably the wife. And Tobias thought the same thing too.

I sat down on the bed to catch my breath.

Tobias sat beside of me.

"I wish we could start over."

"Why?"

"I would've done things differently."

"You still would've been married."

"Yeah. I know. But what if I wasn't?"

I just looked at him. If he hadn't been married to someone else or trying to take me for all of my money, who knows how we would've turned out.

"He's coming. He's really coming," Tobias said.

I could tell that he was excited. I couldn't help but smile.

"I know this might sound crazy. You might think giving me another chance is crazy. You might think that I don't deserve it. But I'm just asking for a chance. A shot to show you that I can be the man that I pretended to be."

"What are you saying?"

Tobias hesitated.

"I choose you. I choose him."

Tobias seemed sad and I wasn't prepared for what he said next.

"We have to get rid of Fran. It's the only way."

What? Never would I have thought that he would say those words. Not about Fran. Not his precious Fran.

"She will never accept him. She will never forgive me."

I thought the opposite of what I assumed that I would be thinking after his comment. My only thought was that if he would turn on the woman that he's been married to for almost twenty years, the woman that knows him, the real him, that has been through hell and high waters with him. If he would turn on her, he would turn on anybody.

"It's the only way. She's not going to stop. I know her. Even after the baby is here. She's not going to stop. So, I have to stop her. He's coming and I have to make sure that he's safe. Strawberry, I'm going to need Ray's number. I'll take care of the rest."

Ray? Oh hell no. We didn't need to involve crazy ass Ray.

"Ray? What are you going to do? Do you really need Ray?"

"That's the only way this is going to work."

~***~

"Look, he just turned on his blue lights," I said to Tobias.

We were on our way to the hospital. A police followed close behind us. Tobias pulled over.

I glanced at the time. We were scheduled to be there in less than thirty minutes.

"Good evening officer. Was I speeding?"

He looked inside of the car.

"No. License and registration please."

Tobias looked at me and I pointed to the glove department. We were driving my car, instead of his. My car already had the car seat in it, ready for the baby.

"I'll be back," the cop said.

He walked away and Tobias told me to call the doctor and let him know that we might be a few minutes late.

"Sir, I need you to step out of the vehicle."

Tobias looked at him like he was speaking some kind of foreign language or something.

"For what?"

"I ran your name and Tobias Fields has an outstanding warrant."

I became nervous and I watched Tobias's reaction.

"A warrant? For what?"

"Assault and Battery."

The officer motioned for him to get out of the car.

"Damn it Fran!" Tobias screamed and hit the steering wheel. The officer drew his gun.

"Get out of the car Sir."

The cop placed the handcuffs on Tobias and he looked as though he was going to kill somebody. The officer patted him down and asked me if I wanted his belongings. I didn't say anything, so finally, the officer just led Tobias away. The police car pulled off, and Tobias looked back at me, sadly, through the window.

They drove away and then I got out and drove myself to the hospital.

Alone.

~***~

"Do you have a name yet?"

"No."

I couldn't stop smiling. I had a son. And I loved him to the moon and back already.

I stared into his big brown eyes. He looked so much like Tobias, but he had my eyes and a cute little button nose. He was mine. He was all mine.

I was going to be a damn good mother to him too. Tobias crossed my mind. He'd missed the birth. I couldn't help but think about him. He was probably going crazy. If nothing else, I knew that he'd wanted to be there. But his wife made sure that wouldn't happen. I'd been in labor for a day and a half, and the phone was in my purse. I wasn't sure if he'd tried to call me from jail or not.

The nurse finished checking me and stated that she was going to take the baby to the nursery for a little while. Just so I could get a little rest. I was in labor for over 36 hours and I needed it. I was so tired. I really needed it.

She let me kiss him and then she took him away.

I rolled over and faced the window. Despite everything, I felt good. I felt really, really, good.

I closed my eyes, hoping to get some rest before Mama made her way back to the hospital to finish spoiling the baby.

"Mrs. Fields?"

I really needed to change my last name.

I turned around. There was a woman standing there in a black suit.

Oh hell.

She shut the door.

"I'm from Child Welfare Services."

"I know."

I looked at her. I couldn't place her but she looked familiar. I felt like I'd seen her before.

"So, as you know, we are going to run a few test on the baby. Everything will turn out fine right?"

"Yes. I have no idea where it came from last time. I don't do drugs. I wouldn't dare take Penicillin knowing that it could kill me. I can't explain it. But I would never hurt my baby."

"Well, we will let you know if anything is found and I guess we will go from there."

She smiled and headed out of the room. I looked at the door for a while and then I closed my eyes.

Suddenly I jumped up!

"Nurse!"

I screamed and pressed the button.

I remembered the woman. She was the one that had come into the hospital room one time before…as "Nurse Jacky". The nurse that they said didn't work there. She'd changed her hair and put on some make-up and glasses. But that was her. That was her! I remembered. She'd been the one to ask me what I was allergic to. Was she involved with the drugs being found in my system somehow?

"Nurse!! Nurse!!"

I got out of the bed just as the nurse came into the room.

"My baby. I think something is going to happen to my baby."

"What? Calm down. He's safe. Come on. Let's get you back in bed."

She tried to get me to calm down, but I continued towards the door.

"What's going on here?"

A woman wearing a blue dress, holding a folder, looked at us suspiciously.

"Let me guess. You are from Child Welfare right?"

"That's right. You were expecting us correct?"

I ignored her, jerked my arm away from the nurse and I ran full speed all the way to the nursery. I burst through the double doors and I looked for him.

I looked for my baby.

But he was gone.

~***~

Shelly sat beside of me.

"I'm so sorry this happened."

I didn't say anything to her.

"Let me help you."

"You can't help me. I just want my baby. Where is my baby?"

The hospital cameras caught the woman pretending to be the Child Welfare agent, taking off her jacket, placing on a nurse jacket and then going into the nursery. The next time she came out, she was carrying a bag. My baby was in that bag. Outside cameras saw her get into a taxi. The taxi had been reported stolen earlier that day. The woman seemed to have dropped off of the map. No one at the hospital even knew who she was. But after looking at footage, they found that she'd been there plenty of times.

Dressed as a nurse. Speaking to patients. And visiting the medicine supply room every single time that she was there.

"I just won't my baby back."

Shelly looked at me.

"Where is Tobias?"

"In jail. He was picked up a few days ago. On our way to the hospital. His wife pressed assault charges on him. I gave the police his name and told them everything that has been going on for the last few months. I told them everything. He's probably going nuts! I hope he at least told them who she was or where she might take the baby. I'm going to go see him. I just want my baby back. I just want my son back."

Shelly grabbed my phone and typed something in it.

"I've been around Brian long enough to learn a thing or two. I did some digging. This is the address to the apartment that Tobias and his wife are renting. Maybe you will get lucky and she's there," Shelly said, and before she could completely close her mouth, I was headed out the door.

I pulled up to the apartment. It was small but it was about thirty minutes from my house. It was in a really expensive neighborhood.

The white Mercedes wasn't there, but a white van was. I knocked on the door. A man in overalls opened it.

"Hi. I was looking for my friend. Fran." I was sure that she probably didn't go by that name, but it was the only one that I knew from Tobias calling her that. If he had a fake name, I was sure that she was going by a fake name too.

"Fran? Yes. That was her name. She lived her with her husband Darren. And her sister. I forgot her name."

Sister? Huh?

"Anyway, they are gone. They moved back East. She'd had someone clear out the place. I didn't get to see him. Just her. She was kind of in a rush."

Back East?

Back East where?

Oh no! My baby could be anywhere by now.

I started to cry and I dropped to my knees. My worst nightmare had come true. My baby was gone. My baby was gone.

~***~

Tobias's Final Say...

I smiled at her. She smiled back.

"I love you," she said.

"I love you too."

She rocked the baby back and forth. She held him close to her but she was wearing a frown. She loved me but would she ever love him? I'd talked her into doing this, and though she didn't want to, she'd did it. She'd did it for me.

As Fran started to feed him, I excused myself and went outside.

The pretend arrest was a good move. I never went to jail. I just wanted Strawberry to think that I did. I hated missing the birth of my son, but in order for things to go smoothly, I had to. Asking Ray for a favor on the whole cop thing was a risk, but I knew that he would do it. He asked one of his cop buddies for a favor, and they actually pulled it off. Of course Ray couldn't be trusted but he didn't have a choice but to cooperate.

I smiled as my other wife pulled up.

Amber. Yep. My second fake-wife, Amber, was still alive. I lied to Strawberry. She wasn't dead. We'd faked her death years ago. The truth is that yeah, initially we were supposed to take her for her money. But as I said, she fell in love with me. She loved me like crazy, and I just couldn't go through with it. So, I told her the truth. I told her about Fran. And just like I expected, she didn't get mad. She actually wanted to come too. She offered to bring all of her money, fake her death so that we could collect off of her life insurance policy, and after getting Fran onboard, she's been with us ever since.

We were lucky that Amber was in the mix, and no one knew about her. Even when spotted at the apartment, we said that she's Fran's sister. She's helped in plenty of ways too. She was the one pretending to be "Nurse Jacky" and helped out with kidnapping the baby. One day, I left the patio door unlocked so that she could switch out Strawberry's prenatal vitamins, to get the whole Child Welfare thing going. I was going to go that route. I was going to get him taken from her, get custody, and go from there. I thought that was the only way. Until I discovered the truth. A truth that even I didn't see coming. So I switched the plan. This whole kidnapping thing was a part of my plan.

Amber walked towards me, smiling.

"I missed you."

"I missed you too," I said to her. I kissed her. She had been just as loyal as Fran and for a while, I'd thought that we had a good thing going. I thought that this would be forever. But Forever is never too far away.

She headed inside of the house with Fran and the baby.

I looked around. It was almost time. And seeing the blue lights in the distance, I looked at the house and headed into the woods…

~***~

My heart was beating faster than ever. We were about an hour and a half from home but we'd gotten word that a woman fitting Fran's description had been spotted with a baby. I was hoping that it was her.

The police surrounded the small house.

I waited impatiently in Ray's cop car. He was the one that told me that they'd got a tip and asked me if I'd wanted to come along. At first I thought that he was lying and trying to get me alone with him but he wasn't.

The police went into the house and I felt like I could hardly breathe. I waited. And I waited. And I waited.

Finally, out came Fran and the other woman who pretended to be a nurse and the Child Welfare representative. They were both in handcuffs. I waited to see if Tobias would come out next.

I'd gone to the jail. Imagine my surprise to find out that he wasn't there. He had never even been arrested! They didn't have him in the system, so my guess was that he'd pulled a fast one on me to help them kidnap my baby. I should have known that he was up to something. I should have known that he couldn't be trusted. I couldn't wait to see the look on his face.

Finally, an officer came out, holding a blue blanket. I saw it move and I jumped out of the car.

I ran to him. I started to cry as soon as I saw my baby's face. I thought that I was never going to see him again. I held him close to my heart as I waited to see if they brought Tobias out of the house next. But they didn't.

Ray came out.

"He's not in there. And technically, he isn't the one on camera committing the crime, or the one spotted with the baby. They are."

I looked at the cars that held both of the women. Fran, Tobias's wife stared at me. She looked as though she wasn't even sorry. But she didn't have to be. I had my baby and with her behind bars and with Tobias out of my life, I was free.

The medics on site, looked at the baby. He was fine. After they were done, I walked back to Ray's patrol car.

I waited for him to finish up. It took a while, but finally, it was time for us to leave.

"He looks like you."

"Yeah. A little."

Ray sat there. I looked at him. Hoping that he wasn't going to try something crazy.

"I'll always love you Strawberry," Ray said. And he started his patrol car. "But I think that he may love you more," he said. And Tobias appeared out of nowhere.

"What?"

"Get out Strawberry. I have to go," Ray said. Tobias walked over and stood by the door.

"What are you doing Ray?"

"I'm letting you go," he said and he unlocked the door for Tobias to help me out.

"I'm not getting out of this car."

"Please. I'm not going to hurt you," Tobias said.

I looked at Ray.

"Get the hell out of my car Strawberry!" Ray screamed and remembering our last run-in, I got out of his car and Ray drove off as soon as I shut the car door.

"What's going on?"

"I couldn't kill them. I had to find another way."

I looked at him confused.

"I couldn't kill Fran or Amber."

"Amber? Dead, fake wife Amber?"

"Yes that was her. The other woman was Amber. It's a long story. But this was the only way. I told them the plan to kidnap the baby. I needed for them to do a crime. So that they would have to do the time. I didn't need to be in the mix. Even though you assumed I had something to do with it, they were looking for them. Not me. Prison was the only way to get them out of the way."

I didn't know what to say. He lied. Amber, fake-wife #2, was alive the whole time? And helping him? I didn't know what to say.

"I was confused. I'll admit that. But finding out the truth made it all easier."

"What truth?"

"Fran and Brian were sleeping together. Amber told me. She said that it had been going on for a while. She showed me the proof. I couldn't believe it. But it made all of this easier. I just hate that Amber had to go too. But I didn't have a choice. My son was my choice."

It was bound to happen. Again, he thought that he could have it all. Obviously Brian could have all of Fran too.

"I choose you Strawberry. And my son. I choose us."

What made him think that he even had a choice?

"You choose us? You choose me because Fran betrayed you."

"No. Like I said. That just made it easier. You changed me. I told you that before. I meant it. I want more. I want life. I don't want to spend the next twenty years pretending. I want to spend them living. And watching my son grow into a better man than me."

I was at a loss for words.

"Won't they tell your involvement?"

"Where is their proof? I covered my tracks. They can say what they want, but this system only works off of proof. Ray helped me. It wasn't easy to get him onboard, but he didn't have a choice. I'd gotten a video from my wife a long while ago that I knew that I would need. His wife, the one after you, Delilah Phillips, he killed her."

What?

"Fran had been watching him, keeping an eye on him for me and she saw him bury her."

"What?" So that's why she never came back around.

"Fran said that she thinks that she was trying to leave him. She was packing her car and then one time she went into the house, and never came back out. Later, she saw Ray carry out something in a sheet. She followed him. Recorded him burying her. She even went to look to make sure after he was gone. It was Delilah."

Wow! So Ray killed Delilah? Well, I guess he really would have killed me if Tobias hadn't stepped in.

"I told him what I needed. Got him to frame the arrest so that I was away from everything that was about to happen. I called in the tip. And I told him to bring you with him. In return, he never has to worry about anyone seeing that video. No one will ever know his secret. We all got them. I know about yours too."

I looked at him. He couldn't possibly be talking about Jake Dawson. I was afraid to ask. So I didn't.

The baby started to whine.

"Run away with me Strawberry."

I looked at him.

"I've given up everything and everybody that meant something to me. I don't have anybody. You don't really have anything or anybody to go back to. Run away with me."

Tobias reached out his hand.

"Where?"

"Anywhere. And I promise not to pick up anymore wives along the way," Tobias joked.

I looked at the baby and then I looked at him.

Thinking about all that was going on with my sisters, and Ray, and the past year with my job, and everything else that had happened, Tobias was right. I didn't really have anything to go back to. I could spend my money anywhere. I could call and check on Mama from anywhere. April was gone. Shelly had the person that she cared about the most. Brian. I wasn't even going to tell her that he'd been sleeping with Fran. After all, she wouldn't tell me. And as for Ray; good bye and good riddance.

I looked at him. Was I really going to do this?

"By the way, "Darren" is a free man now too," Tobias said.

"Fran divorced you? The real you?"

"Yeah. But she doesn't know it yet. My lawyer has all of that being handled. When she's settled in prison. She will be notified. So, what do you say?"

This is crazy! I mean, this is really crazy!

I tried to get my thoughts together. I thought about life. Past and future. I thought about what I'd promised myself when I left my job. I told myself that I would start living. Maybe it was about that time. I had my son. And if nothing else, I had a man that I knew that would protect him to the end. But could I really forget? Could I really get over everything that he'd done to me?

I shook my head. I would never forget. But I guess it wouldn't kill me to forgive. So, finally I took his hand.

Tobias led me to a car that I'd never seen before.

Hopefully Karma was through with me and with any luck, I was praying that she would never have to visit me again.

"There better not be another wife of yours, hiding somewhere," I said as Tobias buckled the baby in the back seat.

"Nah. I've had one wife, too many. Wouldn't you agree?" Tobias said, getting settled into the driver's seat. He smiled at me and just as the sun started to set, Tobias reached for my hand.

Here, this very moment, is where our story; "Darren" and Tiffany's story, begins. Damn it. I guess I was going to become his wife…again.

****

THE END

****

Well…

"The Hidden Wife: The Revenge" From Fran's Side of the Story Comes late September! Make Sure That You Join My Facebook Group by clicking Link below to keep up with the Release Date!

****

IF YOU ENJOYED THIS BOOK, BE SURE TO DOWNLOAD MY NEWEST RELEASE "THE GOOD LISTENER" BY CLICKING HERE:

https://www.amazon.com/Good-Listener-B-M-Hardin-ebook/dp/B01HTWZPME/ref=sr_1_1?ie=UTF8&qid=1469680283&sr=8-1&keywords=bm+hardin

JOIN MY FACEBOOK GROUP FOR SNEAK PEEKS AND MORE BY CLICKING HERE:

https://www.facebook.com/groups/authorbmhardin/

Author B.M. Hardin's contact info:

Facebook: http://www.facbook.com/authorbm

Twitter: @BMHardin1

Instagram: @bm_hardin

Email:bmhardinbooks@gmail.com

TEXT BMBOOKS to 22828 for Release updates!

List of Author B.M. Hardin's best sellers:

Your Pastor My Husband

The Wrong Husband Part One and Two

Reserve My Curves

Desperate: I'll Do Anything for Love

Dirty Bonds

Check out any of these reads by clicking here:

https://www.amazon.com/s/ref=nb_sb_noss?url=search-alias%3Daps&field-keywords=bm+hardin

Made in the USA
Middletown, DE
20 April 2017